Big Sky

Big Sky

Sharon Farritor Raimondo

LUX ET VERITAS BOOKS

ISBN: 978-1-329-08094-2

Jacket photo by: Jack Nordeen
Author photo: Gina Borer
Text and cover design by R. W. Boeche

Unless otherwise indicated, all Scripture passages are taken from
the Holy Bible, NEW INTERNATIONAL VERSION®. *Copyright*
© *1973, 1978, 1984 by Biblica, Inc.*

When Jesus saw his mother Mary there and the disciple,
John, whom he loved standing nearby, he said to her,
"Woman, here is your son," and to John, "Here is your mother". . .
John 19:26

Dedicated to those who made their lives
by risking them.
In memory of my father Ed.
In honor of my uncle John.
And to the glory of God.

Big Sky

You shall rejoice in all the good things
the Lord your God has given to you and your household.
Deuteronomy 26:11

July 18, 1926.

A man stood, hat in hand, surveying his homestead and trying to figure out a way to pay the bank this month. He had borrowed the money to buy his siblings' shares of the land, and the second his signature dried on the note, so did the sky. The wind hadn't blown for days, and he imagined the cows would be disappointed when they arrived at a dusty, empty water tank. When the business of the morning was done, he decided to back the Model T up to the well, jack it up, and bolt a pulley to the rear wheel. A belt should do the trick, and if the fuel holds out, it should idle all day pumping water. His thoughts were interrupted by a baby's sharp cry. He turned toward the house, where a young girl, Angela, poked her head out the front door, "It's a boy, Daddy!" She scurried back into the darkness before a smile leapt across his face.

He turned his gaze toward the sunrise to gauge the time and say a prayer of thanksgiving for the safe delivery of this third son and sixth child. He had always thought the summer sun peeking over the Nebraska Sandhills was the eye of God. Some mornings, like this one, he felt he had God all to himself, cups of coffee steaming between them. Some days, and more often than not, steaming piles of cow manure were what they shared. Either way he was grateful—you can't run a farm without coffee or crap.

He prayed silently as the earth shed the black cloak of night to birth a sky of orange, red, gold, and blue. Redwing blackbirds saddled a solitary wire fence, primping and scanning the dew-laden grass for breakfast. Breathtaking in its own right, the buffalo grass glistened in the sunlight. Cattle shuffled down a hill along a curving clay path toward their first aggravation of the day.

The man, Fred McCloud, could walk to the barn blindfolded and must have done so because no sooner had he left his post than he had arrived. He swung the door open to find two dirty faces—one pitching hay, the other covered in it.

"Your brother Lee just arrived," he said. "You can go meet him when your chores are done."

Turning back toward the house, he heard his eldest son, John, say, "Don't get too excited, Clete; he won't be able to help us with chores for a while. I'm still waiting on you to get big enough."

"I'm big," Clete protested. "I'm four."

"Don't remind me," said John with the authority and irritation of an eight-year-old.

Glancing toward the pasture, Fred noticed a few cattle gathering to voice their complaints about the lack of water. He approached the front door to the house, peeking in through the screen door, "Angela, I'm going to work on the well. The boys will be in to see Mom and Lee when they're done with chores."

"Sure thing, Dad!" she said, grazing the entryway with a small, dark-haired bundle in her arms, "Lee is just lovely."

"Let Mom nurse him before you go dressing him up," he snapped, half-grateful and half-angry that only one of his six kids might get their fill tonight. "You girls help Mom . . . Let her sleep if she's tired . . . I'll see you at midday."

Beginning to feel the added weight of another mouth to feed, he marched toward the shop across from the barn and took out some frustration on the crank of the Model T's engine. It coughed to life, and when it reached full sputter, he climbed in, bouncing through the yard. He hopped out at the precipice of pasture and peeled the wire back tossing it aside. A few cows looked at him cross-eyed as if this were a joyride rather than a rescue operation.

"Calm down. You'll get your water," he spat. John and Clete were just exiting the barn.

"John," he said. "Come close this gate and then go distract your sisters so Mom can nurse Lee. I want you to make sure Mother gets her rest."

"I thought that's why the neighbor is here?" John challenged.

"Do as you're told," Fred said. Climbing back into the Model T, he mistakenly took a breath from above the manifold. The oil burning off of it stung his throat, and he coughed spit into his sleeve. Without a glance back to confirm John's compliance, he steered toward the cattle tank with a band of curious, tail-swishing followers.

With tense lips, John strode toward the twisted pile of wood and wire, lifted it, and stretched it out as far as it would go. He walked it backward toward the fence, secured the post in place, and hooked the rope latch over it. Stepping up on the lower panel, he scanned the hill to see his dad backing the Model T up to the well. He guessed the project wasn't going as planned by the burst of fire and brimstone floating toward him. Whatever Fred was up to looked like a sweaty commitment that would most likely end up with John down in the well knee-deep in mud. He wasn't about to get his fingerprints on that train wreck.

"I'm not fallin' for that again," John said to the nearest cow.

Smiling, he hopped off the gate and ran toward the house. He was going to meet his brother, and nothing was going to stop him.

John guessed his father hadn't met the baby or checked in on Mom. Because, in John's opinion, Fred neglected his fatherly duties and had a strong aversion to hard work and responsibility. John instinctively turned his thoughts toward Marie, his Mom. John hoped she was okay. He had heard stories about women dying while giving birth to their babies. God help them all if they were permanently left in Fred's care.

If you asked John, and no one ever had, every birth sounded like someone getting killed . . . and not in a merciful manner. He had never told anyone, but labor sounds reminded him of the haunting screams he heard coming from behind the barn the night his cat Mae West found a nest of bunnies. If there was a God, and he hadn't given much serious thought to it, he made a mental note to thank Him for having made him a boy instead of a girl. The way he saw it, John had already dodged a bullet.

The screen door creaked and lightly bounced three times in the frame after he passed through. The chattering of his little sisters and Clete giggling drifted down the hall toward him. As John rounded the corner into the kitchen, he found his siblings: Angela, Elaine, Clete, Lucy, and little Lee, who was wrapped in a flour sack and snuggled in the egg-collecting basket. His tiny face was splotched with red marks, and his head was more than a little pointy. John had seen this feature more than once and imagined it had something to do with the process of birth, though he hadn't figured it all out yet. He hadn't noticed that characteristic on the calves he had watched be birthed, so it was still a mystery to him. Lee's dark hair was slicked back and looked wet. His lips rubbed together, and he mewled small contented sounds.

"Choo!" The baby sneezed, the girls exploded in appreciation, and John wondered if they wet themselves from the excitement. Clete just stood gazing at the bundle. Maybe it was dawning on him that he wasn't the baby boy anymore . . . maybe Clete was falling in love . . . John wondered.

"How's Mom?" he asked no one in particular.

"She's resting," said Angela. "She said she feels good."

"Did Lee eat?" John asked.

"Yes, he was a hungry little boy," she answered without looking John's way.

"Fred says I'm supposed to distract you so Mom can sleep," John said.

"Well we're distracted and mom's asleep. Good job, John," she said smiling. "No wonder Daddy made you boss."

John smiled and grew a couple of inches. "He's a little thing, isn't he?" he said.

"You all were once," announced Tecla Mahoney, the neighbor and midwife, as she entered the kitchen, arms full of wet, bloodied linens. "He'll grow in his time," she said, dropping the laundry on the floor, wiping her hands on her apron, and extracting Lee from the basket. "You kids go play. Come back for lunch when the sun is high," she instructed, shooing Lee's fan club out the front door.

"Bye, Lee, love you," the girls sang.

"Come on, Clete," John said, extending his hand. "Let's go find those kittens behind the shop."

"Oh let's!" said Clete. "We should name one Lee."

"Maybe one Lee is enough for this family." John said.

"I don't think so, John. I don't think I can get enough of him," Clete said.

"You might not feel that way when he's bawling in the middle of the night," John said. "You're right though—he is special. We have a big job being his big brothers. We have to teach him things so the girls don't make him soft."

Clete's eyes grew tenfold. "I want to teach him to jump!"

"Let's let him get a little bigger first," chuckled John. "You can handle the jumpin' when the time comes. I promise."

"What will you show him?" Clete asked.

"Oh, I don't know. Maybe everything else," John said. "Remember, Clete, we can help each other, but you've got to do your own growing no matter how tall your father is," or isn't, he thought.

Clete smiled, thinking about how tall daddy was. John was big and really smart about this stuff. Clete liked having a big brother. And now he knew having a little brother made him happy in a new way. Lee's little blue eyes were like the clearest sky he had ever seen, and somehow Clete knew life would never be the same.

— 2 —

As a good husband, I will love my wife, just as Christ
also loved the church and gave Himself for her.
Ephesians 5:25

"Mary, Jesus, and Joseph!" Marie exclaimed. "Out to the yard, kids. Your father is going to blow us up in a grand explosion so we can go meet the good Lord . . . and right before Lee's birthday." She shook her head at the shame of missing the child's big day and shuttled the children out the door. She held Lee on her hip and a rosary in her hand, held over her heart. No one protested going out into the chilly night air in their sleeping shirts . . . complaining wouldn't change it anyway.

The lighting of the oil lamp was a process respected by the innocent bystanders. Marie and Fred each played a starring role, and no one dared intervene. Fred, the official lighter of the lamp, behaved carelessly, exaggerating his clumsiness, thoughtless to his good wife's sensitivities to fire. Marie, the designated commentator, twitched at every shudder of hand, slip of the match, or slight of the wick. Her heartbeat raced in anticipation from the moment the sun fell behind the hills to the second the wick wiggled to life in the shadows.

The children huddled to her skirt like the branches of a weeping willow tree. Lee made the only sounds, squeaking into the night his disapproval of this odd, chilly nocturnal activity.

John, the senior veteran of this performance, stood apart from the group, kicking dust and gazing at the stars.

"This is taking entirely too long," Marie said. "Fred," she yelled into the darkness. "Fred, what are you up to?"

All eyes peered, ears listened, and minutes passed. The cicadas clicked and sang. Tension rose. John spat.

Soft light flickered on its tiptoes then gained balance and stride.

Mom exhaled as she made the sign of the cross, rosary dangling, "Thank you, Lord."

Just as Jesus calmed the waters of Jericho, He had an immediate soothing effect on Marie. "Come children, go inside . . . it's time to do our reading," she said.

Fred slid out the front door, his lanky frame silhouetted in the glow of his successful ignition.

"You should respect that oil, Fred," Marie warned.

"Ahhh . . . boys let this be a lesson to you . . . If you want praise, die. If you want blame, marry." He reached out for Marie, searching for her backside.

Confident Fred had enough success with the lamp, she scooted out of reach. Lee giggled over the activity. John snaked past them and disappeared down the hall into the kitchen.

"Oh, Fred, you are a pill . . . an ever-loving aggravation. I promise you I won't raise these boys to torment their wives by swimmin' in shallow water like you do . . . I'll teach them to go straight for the deep and be done with it."

Laughter rumbled deep inside him, erupted, and raced toward the canyon. No doubt the cattle started at the sound.

"Ah, Marie, you're a beauty even if you're not a full shilling," he followed his adolescent tribe into the house. "What a lark," he concluded.

"Girls, put the dishes away please and then join John and Clete in the family room. We're reading the book of James tonight, and it's one of my favorites," Marie said. "Lee needs a nappy, and then I'll be right in," she explained even though no one was listening.

Fred trotted down the hall, tickling whichever child got too close. He scooped up Lucy and swung her about the kitchen, singing, "Well, I took a stroll down the old long walk on the day I-ay-I-ay, I met a little girl, and we stopped to talk on a grand soft day I-ay. And I ask you, friend, what's a fella to do? 'Cause her hair was RED, and her eyes were blue, and I knew right then, I'd be takin' a whirl down the Salt Hill prom with a Galway Girl."

Fred landed in his wooden, black-leather rocking chair. Lucy hopped to the floor and ran to help the other girls in the kitchen. Clete asked if he could crawl up on Fred's lap and did. He snuggled up to his dad and stared blankly into the flame of the lamp. John sat on the floor with his back to them and curled his legs up to his chest. He didn't understand why the family had to listen to Mom read the Bible each night—seemed like such a waste of time. He knew Fred didn't pay attention to it either; it may have been the one thing they had in common. At least John's schoolwork was completed, and he could go to bed as soon as this was over. He knew the Bible meant a lot to his Mom, and he reminded himself of that. He sometimes felt guilty about not sharing her faith. Maybe someday he would. Maybe when Fred worked a full day and the rains returned. Maybe then . . .

Everyone made their way into the room as their tasks were completed, and the room filled with whispers. Marie handed Lee to Angela to hold while she read. You could see Angela relished the opportunity to goo-goo at him. Lee sparkled for his sisters and wiggled his little legs and grabbed at Angela's hair. He pulled some of it into his mouth and couldn't seem to decide if it was a good decision. Angela didn't care; everything Lee did was cute.

Marie began reading, "Consider it pure joy, my brothers and sisters, whenever you face trials of many kinds, because you know that the testing of your faith produces perseverance. Let perseverance finish its work so that you may be mature and complete, not lacking anything. If any of you lacks wisdom, you should ask God, who gives generously to all without finding fault, and it will be given to you. But when you ask, you must believe and not doubt, because the one who doubts is like a wave of the sea, blown and tossed by the wind. That person should not expect to receive anything from the Lord. Such a person is double-minded and unstable in all they do."

John turned to make sure his father was listening. Clete sat wide-eyed, but Fred's head was already tilting to the side in search of sleep.

Marie was right last Christmas when she said, "If your father were running the Bethlehem Inn, the holy family would still be wandering the earth." John decided it were true, not because of lack of payment, but because of lack of a manger. Fred would give anything away, no matter how desperately his own family needed it . . . the holy family would wander because Fred would give them poor directions to a building that the neighbors already tore down for fencing.

John looked back to his mother, wondering how on earth she got coupled up to Fred. John had never seen Fred break a sweat from work. Fred claimed he suffered from a form of heatstroke-induced epilepsy. Because John couldn't imagine Fred working hard enough to achieve heatstroke, he suspected he was misdiagnosed. The eldest son had never witnessed one of Fred's seizures; and although he had overheard grown-ups speak of them with horror, he didn't really believe they were that big of a deal. Regardless, John knew he would never understand adults and hoped the secrets to life would lie in this book of promises his mom was intent on sharing with her family.

"For the sun rises with scorching heat and withers the plant; its blossom falls and its beauty is destroyed," she read.

"Tell me something I don't know," John thought.

3

He whose tongue is deceitful falls into trouble.
Proverbs 17:20

"Bless me Father for I have sinned," John said. "It's been three months since my last confession, and in that time I . . . I . . . I . . . yelled at Fred, I've hated Fred, I've wanted to hurt Fred . . . and . . . I've used foul language . . ."

John knew Father Kellen was aware of the confessor's identity, so it was pointless to be subtle.

Silence filled the dark closet. The small privacy screen in front of John spoke, "Is that everything, my son?"

"Umm . . . Let me think about it for a minute . . . ," said John, realizing the opportunity he faced. He wasn't fond of Father Kellen and thought he could have some fun coming up with some creative sins to confess."

"I kicked a chicken to see if it would fly . . . I . . . I . . . made my brother Clete wear my sister's underwear . . . I tasted some whiskey and mixed it in with the horse's water . . ."

As the boy sat thinking of more hideous crimes to boast, Father said, "John, we both know chickens don't fly, and I don't believe you are thick enough to think they might. I believe you are making fun of the sacrament of confession, and that, young man, IS a sin."

John said, "Well, Clete really does wear my sisters' underwear. I didn't think he would enjoy it so much, and my sisters are gonna kill him if he keeps stealing from their drawers." The adolescent sinner cupped fingers over his mouth to stifle laughter. "You wait and see, Father; my story will be confirmed in the confessions of my sisters and maybe even Clete if he's brave enough."

John heard the man of God stand from his chair and the knob of his closet door engage. John stood upright and bolted out the heavy purple curtain that concealed him from other sinners of the flock. Fortunately, the closet door opened toward John so he was hidden from the Father's view for a moment. John had just enough time to slide under the pew beneath his sisters, who were waiting their turn for confession.

"Cover me," John whispered, rolling beneath the pew.

The girls stood and curtsied to Father as he strode past. Hell was bubbling up over his white collar, and he snapped, "Where did that boy go?"

The girls stood looking at each other; Lucy finally spoke, "I'm sorry Father, we were so deep in prayer preparing for our confessions, I guess we didn't notice."

Father Kellen exhaled loudly and cleared his throat. "Well, you tell your mama that I'd like to speak with her before you leave tonight."

"Yes, sir," Angela said. "We will do that. May I confess, Father? I believe I'm ready."

"Of course, Angela," he said, regaining his holy composure.

Angela scooted down the pew, and John lay frozen beneath them. He decided he should try this again when it wasn't his sisters' skirts dangling in front of him. As if Angela realized his offensive idea, she stepped firmly on his fingers and twisted her shoe.

"Thank you, Father Kellen," she said, pushing her heel down.

John's face scrunched up, and he inhaled, biting his lip.

"I certainly appreciate your hearing my confession," she added, stepping off John's fingers.

Father Kellen, forever the gentleman, used his hand to slice the air in front of Angela, guiding her toward the confessional. She smiled, nodded, and stepped toward the curtained entry.

The priest drew the curtain closed and then entered his small area to continue with the evening's services.

When John heard the door latch, he slid from behind the pew and the cover of Lucy's and Elaine's skirts. Rubbing his freshly pressed hand, he leaned forward to whisper to Lucy, "I need you to do something for me . . ."

Lucy could hardly keep a straight face. "John, you are gonna get me in trouble," she said.

"This time it's entirely worth it," John said.

Lucy just smiled, "What?"

"Confess that you get angry with Clete for stealing your underwear," said John.

She gasped and snorted laughter through her fingers. "What? Why would I do that?"

"Just do it," John said. "I'll explain later."

"Do what?" asked Marie as she walked up beside the conspirators.

"She's confessing next," said John. "She gets cold feet."

"Oh Lucy," Marie said. "You are a wonderful child, and this is a way to stay right with God. Honey, you have nothing to worry about."

"Thank you, Mama," said Lucy. "I just don't like the closed spaces."

"Well, it wouldn't kill them to wash those curtains," Marie said. "I will grant you that."

"Mom," John said, "may I go play outside?"

"Are you done?" she asked.

"Yes, ma'am," said John. "I went first."

"What did you get for penance?" she asked.

"I think that's still coming," said John. "He wanted to give it some thought."

"Well, that's unusual," said Marie. "You can play outside but stay close. I'll come for you if Father makes his decision."

"Thank you, ma'am," said John.

He began backing down the aisle, giving Lucy his best puppy dog eyes.

The confessional curtain swung open, and John turned to run outside. Angela sent him a stern look as she knelt to say her penance.

Elaine stood to go next.

13

"Let Lucy go, Elaine," said Marie. "She's nervous."

"Of course," said Elaine.

"It'll be fine, Lucy," said Marie. "You are a child of God, and he dearly loves you."

"Yes, Mama," Lucy said.

Lucy swung the purple curtain back and noticed the mildewy scent escaping from its creases. She knelt on the small bench, placed her hands together, and began, "Bless me father for I have sinned. It's been three months since my last confession, and in that time I have been envious of beautiful dresses and nice homes, and I've wished for our circumstances to improve at home, full-well knowing that the good Lord will provide everything that I need."

"Is that everything, my child?" asked Father Kellen.

She took a deep breath. "Well, there is one thing that is terribly embarrassing. I'm not sure how to say it without losing your respect, Father."

"Our God grants forgiveness through me for all sins truly repented," he said. "I am an instrument of God, and I do not judge, my child. It's best to relieve yourself of the weight of the sin now before it grows into something more."

"Thank you, Father," she said. "I get angry sometimes at my brother Clete. He is very small, and I know I should be more patient with him."

"Children can be trying," Father Kellen added.

"Well, Clete continues to sneak away with . . . with . . . ," she said, clearing her throat and trying not to let laughter crack her voice into pieces. "He takes my undergarments from my room, and it makes me very angry."

Silence filled the confessional, and Lucy covered her mouth with her hands. She leaned forward, brushing her hair against the privacy screen. She waited for a response; and hearing nothing, she began to feel incredibly frightened about going along with John's joke.

"Father?" she asked. "Are you there?"

"I am," he said. "Lucy, did your brother John tell you to confess this?"

She couldn't hold the laughter in anymore, and it exploded into the darkness.

"Child, child . . . calm down. I'm not saying it isn't true. I just had to be sure," Father said.

Lucy inhaled, deeply confused by what he was saying.

"Don't cry, my child," he said. "Are you comfortable with me talking to your mother about it, or would you like to visit with her?"

Clearing her throat again, she said, "Oh, I can visit with my mama about it. I just wanted to confess my anger." Pulling herself together, she said, "I am sorry for these sins and all the sins of my life. I ask for forgiveness, absolution, and penance."

"Say, three Our Fathers and two Hail Maries and sin no more," Father Kellen said.

He began praying softly through the privacy screen, and Lucy was already feeling guilty. Even still, it was funny.

It took the rest of the evening to get the family through the confessional; and just before loading up in the Model T, Father Kellen called down the steps of the church to Marie.

"May I have a word?" he asked.

"Of course," she said.

John and Lucy exchanged worried glances.

"What's going on with them?" asked Fred looking from face to face for clues.

Clete stood on the front seat, "Maybe he wants me to confess."

"Son, you're too young to have done anything," said Fred. "You'll get your turn, and then it will be never ending. You can confess every day if you want."

"Really?" Clete asked.

"Really," Fred said.

The family could see Marie exhale by her body language, and she reached out a gloved hand to shake Father Kellen's. She nodded to him and turned toward the vehicle. Her face seemed firm yet not angry. John was confused. He had expected something more dramatic. Father Kellen stood on the steps of the cathedral sending John prayers of exorcism or salvation . . . he couldn't be sure. John knew by Marie's silence that he may have crossed a line. He knew by her silence that this was going to be painful.

"Is everything ok?" asked Fred, as she took her seat.

"It will be," she said.

Fred nodded, "This, children, is what you call a need-to-know situation. It is apparent that we do NOT need to know."

"Any stops at the church outhouse before we hit the road?" Fred asked.

"Nope," everyone said in unison.

"Let's go," Fred said, pushing the gearshift into first and bouncing through the churchyard toward the road.

Clete crawled up into Marie's lap, and Fred caught John's eye in the rear view mirror. Neither spoke, but John knew the jig was up. It was a matter of time before his underwear stunt would redden his backside. It was incredibly strange that no one was yelling at him. Usually, Fred and Marie took turns lecturing him, and Fred acted as though he had no idea what was going on. John knew this wasn't good. Marie was up to something.

Lucy sat sweating in her seat for her involvement and wouldn't even look at John. Angela and Elaine were in their own little world, reveling in the refreshing lightness of their souls.

After a late supper and a quick read from the book of Philippians, Marie and Fred disappeared into their bedroom. The girls giggled with Clete, and John sat realizing that the anticipation of punishment may be more uncomfortable than the actual act.

When the bedroom door opened, Fred called out, "John, can you come into the kitchen please?"

John stood. Lucy paused, sending him fearful condolences.

John entered and stood by the kitchen table.

"Please take a seat, son," he said.

John paused; usually Marie handled the punishments. They were pulling out all the stops. This can't be good.

"Father Kellen brought it to our attention that there is a pattern developing in your confessions," Fred said. "Do you know what I'm talking about?"

"No, sir," John said.

"He said that you confessed hateful thoughts toward me," Fred said. "Is it true that you feel this way?"

"Sometimes," John said. "I thought confession was private."

"It is," said Marie. "We don't know anything specific about your conversation. Father is just concerned that you may actually hurt your dad, and he wanted us to be aware."

"Oh," said John, in part angry at this new development and partly relieved that Clete's alleged fetish wasn't being discussed.

"Son," Fred said. "I love you. I always have and I always will. It is pretty clear that we are unique people with varied approaches to life and different personalities. But son, there is nothing wrong with our differences. If we were all the same, life would get pretty boring. I really need you to understand that I love you and that you are a gift to me from God. Marie and I prayed for a child, and He gave us you. We are grateful for that every day."

John looked at his shoes. "Well, I'm sorry that I get upset sometimes."

Fred reached out to John and drug the boy toward him for a hug. "We all get upset sometimes, John," he said. "I just ask that when you get upset with me, you talk to me about it so we can fix things. Okay?"

"Okay," said John. "Is that all?"

"Well, you should know that when I was your age, I had a temper too. I was red faced well into my twenties. Just ask your mother. She's seen it, and she can see you've inherited my passion. That's all I need to say," said Fred. "Marie?"

Marie sat looking at John with flat features. "John," she said, "I volunteered you to be an altar boy on Sunday."

"What?" John said. "Why in the heck would you do that?"

"Would you like me to tell you why, or would you like to wear a little red dress for a day and pretend the rest of this evening didn't happen?" she asked.

John thought about it. "Fine," he said.

"If you mock my church or its sacraments again, young man, this will become a weekly responsibility," she said. "Clear?"

"Yes, ma'am," John said.

"Now get to bed," Marie said. "Would you ask Lucy to come see us?"

John threw his face upward and stepped toward the family room. "Lucy," he said. "I'm sorry . . . your turn."

Lucy stood and hugged John on the way by. "It was pretty funny," she whispered.

The young girl entered the kitchen meekly. "John said you wanted to see me," she said.

"Have a seat," said Fred. "Marie's gonna do the talking. Okay? . . . Don't worry," he whispered, "I think it's a lark."

"Fred," said Marie, glaring and then dissolving into giggles.

The sound of John's bedroom door slamming upstairs echoed down the stairway.

Lucy sat confused. "Am I in trouble?" she asked.

"Yes," laughed Marie.

Fred shook his head no.

"What is going on with you two?" Lucy asked.

"John will hear, Marie. Calm down," said Fred.

Marie pulled herself together. "Okay, Lucy, we know John put you up to his little joke on Father Kellen (who, by the way, bought it hook, line, and sinker). John is in big trouble for some other things that happened at church and for mocking the act of confession. You are guilty of that sin as well. We can't let John know how funny we thought it was, because that would only encourage him. It is troublesome the lack of faith that boy displays, so we came down pretty hard on him. He's going to be an altar boy on Sunday."

Lucy gasped, "Really? Can I go watch him?"

"We're all going to watch," said Fred. "Front row seats. We can't miss a beat of that."

Marie started again, "But, to be fair, you need to be punished as well, so I would like you to wash the confessional curtains for Father

Kellen next week. They are heavy and it will be a tough job, but I will make sure that John helps you too. And not a single word to John about our laughter. Agreed?"

"Yes, ma'am," said Lucy.

"Now get to bed and please don't let John get you in trouble again," said Marie. "God does not appreciate his church being run down."

"Yes, ma'am," said Lucy. "Thank you."

Fred hollered out, "Oh, I'll get a lock for your chest of drawers, too."

Marie cackled. Lucy's smile erupted, and she sprinted up the stairs to bed.

As she passed John's bedroom, she found John peeking out the door. "Are you okay?" he asked.

"Yes," she said. "Are you?"

"I have to be an altar boy," said John. "I'm not sure it was worth that."

Lucy started laughing. "I think it was entirely worth it," she said. "Good night, John," she said, kissing his cheek.

"'Night, Lucy," he said. "Hey, what did you get?"

"I have to wash the confessional curtains," she said. "You get to help."

John's head fell forward, "Ugh."

Lucy waved at her melancholy brother and gently closed her bedroom door behind her.

4

Whatever you do, work heartily, as for the Lord and not for men,
knowing that from the Lord you will receive the inheritance
as your reward. You are serving the Lord Christ.
Colossians 3:23-24

John spent the next three days dreading the little red dress he would wear on Sunday. He had tried to build a reputation of being tough, and the thought of his school mates seeing him prancing around in a little God gown made him feel sick.

Worse than that, he worried Lois Johnson would see him. Lois was his best friend at school, and he knew she would enjoy watching him serve the Lord . . . whom he was beginning to dislike as much as his earthly father. John and Lois shared a bench seat desk in the third row at District 222. There had been more than one moment that John imagined them sharing a bench as little gray-haired adults. Lois was a beauty, inside and out. She could see right through John's roughness and speak to the soft, squishy part of his heart that he kept hidden from the world. Just the thought of Lois laughing at him was punishment enough for his crime.

John's only saving grace, as he saw it, was that it was the last Sunday of Catholic summer school, and there would be thirty altar boys serving with him. He hoped he could blend in to the glorious gaggle of gowns. In his heart, he knew he would stand out like a mule among stallions.

John tolerated the comments and encouragement his family was tossing his way and did so with an even temperament. He tried to act as if it didn't bother him; but when no one else was around, he found himself bowing and genuflecting like he'd seen the regular altar boys do. He wanted to blend in, and so he ran church memories through his mind as much as he could, practicing the motions whenever taunting eyes weren't looking.

Finally, Sunday reared its ugly head, and the McClouds loaded up in the Model T to get to services. To John's dismay, the family left early so that John could be there in plenty of time to prepare for his responsibilities. John felt sick. He wanted to vomit and found himself swallowing the awful taste of a load denied more than once.

Unloading from the car, Lucy put her arm around him and said, "John, it will be fine. Go in the back door and no one will see you. You'll blend in. I promise."

John nodded. "Good idea," he said.

"Good luck, John," Marie said. "Make me proud."

"Sure," he said, swallowing the taste of vomit again.

He walked around the church toward the back door and glanced toward the outhouse. He considered using the facilities before going in but decided if he got in there, he may never come out. Mrs. Lantis saw him loitering in the backyard and pulled him inside the church.

"Let's get you dressed," she said.

Hanging on a hook were a red gown and a little white blouse. Mrs. Lantis removed John's coat and tried to hurry John along. "We don't have much time to get lined up," she said.

John looked down the hall to find the other twenty-nine sorrowful souls packed into the church's back room like sardines. None of them spoke, and half of them looked as disappointed as John felt. John pulled the red gown over his head, and Mrs. Lantis topped it off with the blouse. John felt like a strawberry sundae.

John joined his fellow servants and felt ill. He swallowed hard and realized that he may be worried about the wrong end. Mrs. Lantis lined them up shoulder to shoulder. She gave the front guy a cross on a stick to carry, and the one next to him hauled an empty bowl and a blessed napkin.

Mrs. Lantis led the pack out the back door and around to the front of the church, where they found Father Kellen waiting. The organ boomed from inside the cathedral, and Father Kellen said a prayer for the mass and for those serving during it.

John tried to disguise a rumble in his stomach by clearing his throat. He felt weak and realized the bathroom break would have been prudent prior to getting into his scarlet getup.

John followed the boy ahead of him when he moved and felt like a milk cow on the clay path at home. They entered the church, and John was grateful that he could only see the faces of those seated near the aisle. As Father Kellen approached the altar, John's stomach growled as if a demon were trying to escape. The boy next to John glanced his way and asked, "Are you okay?"

"Yeah," John whispered. "Just nervous, I guess."

The red-and-white faithful knelt down in front of the altar with hands closed in prayer for the first thirty minutes of the service. The boy with the bowl and napkin stood and took it to Father Kellen after another altar boy rang a bell. John thought the kid looked ridiculous, before realizing he was currently the boy's twin.

John began feeling very hot, then cold, sweaty, and clammy. He realized the cork he had imagined placing in his backside was about to burst out. He stood as slowly and cautiously as he was able and bowed to the altar to try to make his exit look official. He walked with his hands clasped and his cheeks clenched all the way across the front of the church. He exited through a side door; and once out of sight of the congregation, he ran out the back, his gown waving in the wind. He ripped open the outhouse door to find the seat covered in piss and shit. He knew he wouldn't be able to act quickly enough to save him from getting it all over himself, so he bypassed the outhouse stool and flew into the weeds behind it.

John's fingers flew to unfasten his pants, and he squatted in the nick of time. It was the most satisfying bowel movement of his life. He took his time to make sure he was finished. As he squatted, he decided the people of this church would never be able to find the gates of heaven since they obviously couldn't find a ten-inch hole that sat two feet in front of them. He had never realized the holy outhouse was in such a sad state.

John could hear people exiting the church and knew he needed to get back in to finish his punishment, or Marie and Fred may make him do this again.

As the boy stood, he realized he made a grievous error. Because he wasn't accustomed to wearing a skirt, he hadn't taken the time to get it out of the way. He had covered the inside of his gown with loosey-goosey diarrhea. Panicking, John tried to wipe it clean on the ground. He had a handkerchief in his pocket that he used to clean his backside. He carefully removed the gown and blouse from over his head, pulled up his pants, and folded the gown up with the dirty parts hidden.

Mrs. Lantis found him walking toward the back door.

"Just hang that up, John," she said. "Good job today."

"Thank you, Mrs. Lantis," he said.

The other boys had already escaped, and so John found himself alone in the back room. He hung the soiled gown and blouse up on a hanger and slid it into the closet with the other twenty-nine spotless gowns.

Father Kellen came up behind him.

"Thank you, John," he said. "You should think about helping us out more often. We could use you."

"Thank you, Father," John said. "I'll consider it."

"You do that," said Father. "God bless. Tell your mama thank you, too."

"I will," John said, walking backward into the church to escape.

John picked up the pace, hoping the smell wouldn't grab Father's attention before he could get away. He sniffed his hands and realized he still smelled guilty. As he passed the fountain of holy water at the door, John dipped his hands in and rinsed. He dried his hands on a woman's skirt as he walked through the crowd and found his family waiting for him at the Model T.

"Where did you go?" Marie asked.

24

"Father had me doing some things behind the scenes," John said.

"Oh," she said. "Were you ringing the bell?"

"Yes," said John. "Can we go now?"

Fred laughed, "Yes, let's go home."

The McClouds loaded up, and Fred steered the vehicle out onto the road. John looked nervously over his shoulder until the church was out of sight.

"So," Lucy asked, "how was it?"

"Not bad," said John. "I feel pretty good."

"I knew you would do great," said Marie. "I bet they'll ask you to serve again in the future."

"I don't know about that," said John.

"Why wouldn't they?" Marie asked.

"No reason," said John.

And to Marie's disappointment, and John's relief, no one called on him to be an altar boy ever again.

5

I will not be afraid in any man's presence,
for the judgment is God's.
Deuteronomy 1:17

Little Joey arrived in the traditional way, although he dared begin his journey into the world on a Friday and didn't finish the trip until early Saturday morning. From the start, Marie was concerned about him because of an Irish legend, which predicted that if a person started something on a Friday that couldn't be finished that same day, it brought bad luck. However, if you continued the project through the weekend and finished it on Monday or later, the bad luck would pass your home as if sheep's blood stained the door frames. Marie later swore that if she had realized it were Saturday when Joey crowned, she would've tied her legs together and hung from the ceiling until Monday, when it was safe for her to deliver him.

The girls had not outgrown their love for children and pampered the tot at all times. Lee had a hard time welcoming Joey because he didn't see what the fuss was all about. Sure Joey was cute. Piglets were cute too, but Lee knew how ugly they became when grown. The new baby was cutting into his playtime, and Lee noticed everyone smiling at Joey instead of him. The recently ousted youngest child went about his business, hoping it would all blow over.

After Joey's birth Fred seemed overwhelmed by the smallest offense. It had gotten so bad that after dropping a sugar bowl and breaking it, John decided he would run away. He talked Elaine into going with him, since she was a witness and, in John's absence, would surely take the heat. The allegedly guilty pair trekked over the hill to George Eblin's sod house, where they sat on a bench trying to decide their next move.

The Eblins were a jovial old pair who fed the runaways potatoes and gravy and asked no questions. George was a wise man of many talents. He was born in 1860 and was a legendary butcher. George was also a doctor and veterinarian and, as a young man, a quality hunter. Now, at sixty-eight years old, the man couldn't see, hear, or lift much weight; but he didn't let these challenges interfere with his cutting or doctoring. A rumor floated around the hills that after trying to cut a pig's jugular vein, George left the animal to retrieve a tool from another building. When he returned, the hog was out in the pen, eating slop that proceeded to fall right out its opened throat. The owner of the hog separated it from the others, corralled it in the shed, and then shot it so that it wouldn't suffer any longer. Outside the cost of the bullet, which George deducted from his fee, and the storytelling rights (free of charge), George butchered the animal as usual. Apparently, the pig's owner claimed it was the best pork loin his family had ever tasted. Despite the tremendous flavor, the butchering business slowed down a great deal for George since that appointment.

The sun went down over the valley; and although John had never slept in a soddy (which he wasn't interested in doing), he certainly didn't feel like sleeping outside a soddy (which Elaine swore would be the end of her). At an impasse, George volunteered his adult nephew, who had been staying with them, to walk them home.

Before the kids left, George asked John, "How old are you, son?"

"Ten," John said.

"Knowing it's none of my business, I'm going to give you some friendly advice. Is that okay with you?" he said.

"Ummm, sure." John said.

"The reasons you had for leaving home will remain until you deal with them. Don't fool yourself into thinking that because you're only ten, you aren't able to stand as a man. You are a McCloud. You're a good man, and you work harder than a lot of men in these parts. Be proud of that. Be proud of who you are. Don't forget your mama loves you. Do you understand what I'm saying?"

"Yes, sir," John said. "Thank you, sir."

Suddenly ashamed that a broken sugar bowl brought him to abandon his family, John was ready to face his punishment. Everyone said goodbye, and John never forgot the handshake he shared with George. John had no idea that George, or anyone, thought so highly of him. He also didn't realize that people were aware of his father's struggles and illness. He couldn't decide which piece of information made him happier but felt relieved to be going home.

On the walk home, Elaine made small talk about coyotes and snakes. John, hands in pockets, parted the field a different person.

⤙ 6 ⤚

I will watch, stand fast in the faith, be brave, and be strong.
1 Corinthians 16:13

June 1, 1928.

Ten-month-old Joey is sleeping under a coat on his parents' bed. His cheeks are bright red, and his fingers grip one another in an orchestrated tangle as if in prayer. Soft, contented sounds escape him as he readjusts to his side, legs splayed and half of his face buried in the quilt.

In the next room, Marie sits rocking in Fred's big leather chair, mumbling to the click of her rosary beads. The quiet was a treat she didn't indulge in very often. The other children were playing at the neighbors, and Fred was out tinkering on something she knew was two repairs beyond hope. She rose to check on Joey. Peeking through the door, she saw he had all but kicked off the blanket she covered him with. His infant frame was awkward—a long torso and short legs; and he always slept with his hands folded. He would grow into himself, just as the others had. The good Lord would see to that. He wasn't facing her, but his chest rose and fell as it should, so she decided to start dinner.

She glanced out the window, looking for Fred. She found his legs jutting out from under the wagon. She didn't realize anything needed fixing on it. Watching him, she noticed he lay still. After a moment without movement, fear mounted; she bolted out of the bedroom and through the front door.

"Fred, are you alright?" she said.

There was no answer.

Fearing he may have had a seizure, she ran to him. She grabbed his boots and started pulling with all of her weight, trying to drag him out where she could see him. He started, jumped, and kicked, "What the hell?" he said as his head hit the bottom of the wagon.

"Are you sleeping under there?" Marie asked, throwing his boots to the ground.

"Well I was. Now I just have a headache," he said, scooting out from the wagon's shade and shielding his eyes from the bright sun.

"I thought you had a seizure! Lord, help me. Have you gotten any work done?"

"Enough," he said.

"The kids will be home soon. I'm making supper," she said.

"Fine, I'll finish up."

Marie turned, rolling her eyes, galled at what he could possibly need to "finish" up.

"Lord, give me patience . . . ," she said, turning toward the house.

Making her way to the kitchen, she poured some water in the pot on the stove and tossed a bit of salt in. She turned to the sink and began peeling potatoes. She loved peeling potatoes. There was something soothing about the sound the peeler made as it worked. She missed the full, heavy potatoes of Ireland. The potatoes they were able to grow here would be laughed out of the kitchens of Kilkenny. Back home, it was a man for every potato, and he'd have some left to feed the dog. Here it took at least five to equal a serving. However, there are advantages to smaller potatoes. They boiled quicker, were easier to store and mash, and came out of the ground more readily. However, they didn't taste as good as the average Ireland crop. More butter was required, which given the dryness of the milk cow, they were learning to live without.

It always amazed Marie how one variable of life could impact so many others. No rain meant no crop, no milk, and more work. That meant less coffee, less washing, less bathing, less boiling, and a husband who needed more understanding and more encouragement. She reminded herself that God never said life would be easy but that it will be worth it.

"Amen," she said aloud.

"Are you praying for me again?" Fred asked. He sauntered up behind her at the sink. Wrapping his arms around her waist, he lay his head on her shoulder, "I'll take all I can get. Don't forget to ask for rain and a way to fix the lister. Oh, and a fix for the bump on me head."

"Oh, Fred, you know I never stop praying for you," she said.

"Good. But I'm gonna hold your hand pretty tight as we cross St. Peter's threshold . . . just in case."

She smiled, "Well, you should be nice to me, or I'll announce you're following me and I don't know you from Adam."

"Ha! That's a hoot," he said. "Marie, we said, 'til death do us part.' You're a free bird once I'm called home. But I'm certain you won't know what to do without me."

"The kids and I will join the circus. It's the one thing we're trained for. And by the way, you should enjoy that bump on your noggin— you earned every bit of it."

"Och, ouch. I'm hurt, Marie," he said, smiling and rubbing his head.

"Will you wake Joey? It always takes him a bit to come around to eating after a nap."

"Sure Marie," he said, pecking her shoulder before turning away.

After two or three steps he said in a suggestive voice, "You know, the kids aren't home yet . . ."

"Fred McCloud, I have potatoes to start boiling and an infant sleeping in our bed. We haven't time for your fancy today," she said. The sound of the potato peeler continued its pace, and Marie didn't turn his way.

"Och, Marie. Me heart may never recover . . . losing you to boiling potatoes . . . ," he said. Dramatically, he clenched his chest as if shot by an arrow and fell back a few feet into the kitchen wall. One hand swung out to the wall, and he slid down to the floor like molasses, whimpering all the while.

"You seem to have a lot of energy, Fred. Perhaps it is a good day to patch that hole in the roof," she said, turning to him and smiling, potato peeler silent.

"Must wake the babe, Marie; you know how he is about eating right after a rest," he said, slipping through the bedroom door.

The potato peeler began its rhythmic song and echoed down the hall.

A few potatoes later, the children began filing into the house, Clete first, then Elaine, Lucy, Lee, John, and Angela.

Their chatter drowned out the chef's instrument, and Marie turned to welcome them back and ask how their day at the neighbors' house went.

Suddenly the bedroom door swung open. "Marie, come here," Fred said. "Now."

Marie jumped toward the bedroom, peeler in hand, "What's wrong? What's wrong with my baby?"

Fred pulled her in and quickly shut the door.

The children were silent. "Joey . . . Joey . . . wake up, honey . . . ," they heard Marie say through the door. Then, she screamed. The potato peeler hit the floor. "No, Lord, no," she said, collapsing, Joey in her arms. Her tears running down his face, joining the trail of blood that fell from the infant's ear, like a tributary joining a river. She rocked the child in her arms, burying her face in the bundle of him. Fred stood silent.

In the kitchen, tears were falling from every eye. Even Lee, who didn't quite understand what was happening, wept. Angela picked him up and held him tightly. The other girls huddled around Angela and Lee, sobbing. Clete went to John's side and reached up for his hand. John held it firmly, tears frozen on his cheeks, staring at the bedroom door, listening to his mom wail.

"Everyone, outside," said John. "Let's give them some space."

Like turtles, the group gathered the will and focus to get moving. Angela ushered the girls down the hall, and John followed them, pushing Clete ahead.

"If Joey is sick, we need to be strong for Mom," John said in the most encouraging voice he could muster. "She will need us . . . " he said.

Walking down the hall toward the front porch, John heard the bedroom door open behind him. The girls continued moving toward the door, and he stopped to look back. His dad stood holding the doorknob, facing the floor, listening to Mom's tortured cry. Dad felt John's gaze and looked toward him with dry eyes. For a moment, John felt they connected.

Fred brought his hand up to his face, covered his eyes, and walked out of John's field of vision. He picked up the telephone from the east wall of the room and asked for Father Kellen.

John understood at that moment that Joey wasn't sick but in fact was dead. Otherwise, Dad would've asked for Doc Stone.

"Can we go see Mommy?" Clete asked.

"No, not now. She's upset," said John. "Let's go hug the girls. They need us too. Come on," he said.

Pushing the screen door open, John could feel the coolness of evening coming up from the valley. The cicadas sang, the hills rolled, and the girls huddled on the step. Lee had recovered and was drawing in the dirt with a stick. Clete let go of John's hand and ran to the girls, who immediately absorbed him into their cocoon.

John listened to his mom's forsaken howl travel down the hall toward him. He imagined the sound floating through the valley, and he wondered if the cattle understood what it was. Did the prairie dog, bird, and snake mothers recognize the sound of another mother losing her child? He decided they didn't.

The children waited for the house to grow quiet.

"I'm gonna check on them," said Angela.

She entered the house, and Clete, Elaine, and Lucy held each other on the step. Lee continued to play in the dirt, and John looked out over the valley.

Lee decided he needed a diaper change and headed toward the house. He met Elaine at the door, who was happy to help him out of his wet pants and into something fresh and dry. She decided Lee didn't need to hear so many tears falling, so she took him and Clete out to a stone bench near the small, round, gray cement-block building used for storing water. The trio sat there watching the sun drop beneath the hills of the valley.

Lucy went inside the house and paused at the bedroom door. Mom stood facing the window, her shoulders shaking. Angela had her arm around her waist and her head leaning toward her shoulder. She couldn't see Joey but saw a small dish towel on the bed, with a small red stain. She could see Dad's big arms wrapped around a bundle, as he stared at it, chewing his bottom lip ravenously. He looked up at Lucy, and tears streamed down his sun-dried face. The droplets of pain left trails of clean skin, making his dirt dusting look darker. He made no sound. His head fell forward, and his fingers obsessively rubbed the edge of Joey's swaddling. The chair rocked with effort, causing the pine-wood floor to cry a mournful song. Realizing as John had earlier that Joey wasn't sick at all, she ran down the hall, threw open the door, and tackled John from behind.

"He's dead, John! He's dead! Joey's dead!" she cried, burying her face into his neck.

John said nothing but wrapped her in his arms. They held each other as the sun fell. Seeing nothing but the face of their little brother as they had seen him last: happy, playful, and smiling.

Soon enough, the sound of the cicadas was joined by the sound of Fred's boots down the hall. He stepped through the screen door and paused. The door bounced in the frame, and they turned to look at him. "Joey must have died in his sleep," he said.

No one spoke. Dad's boots moved, and his shoulder brushed John on the way past. "I'm going to make a box," he whispered.

He strode past Lee, Elaine, and Clete, who had gathered at the foot of the house. Small clouds of dust followed him toward the shop.

Almost immediately upon arriving in the shop, the sound of a saw chewing through wood rose into the night.

7

Yea, though I walk through the valley of the shadow of death,
I will fear no evil; for You are with me;
Your rod and Your staff, they comfort me.

Psalm 23:4

June 2, 1928.

Marie held Joey for hours. She wrapped him in a blanket and rocked him in Dad's chair. She didn't speak to anyone. Occasionally she burst into tears, mumbled, and then grew quiet. She dozed off cradling him; and when she woke, she started to unwrap him for a nappy change. As she realized her nightmare wasn't a dream, she erupted.

Fred entered the dark room and said, "It's time to put him down, Marie."

She lifted her head, brushed her hair from her face, and answered him with her eyes.

Fred backed out of the room, shut the door, and let his temple rest on the closed door.

After a moment, he called the children together and announced his plan.

"Mom needs more time with Joey," he said. "Angela, Elaine, and Lucy, you'll be on duty with Mom tomorrow, caring for Lee and handling meals. Get up early. Elaine, can you find something soft for Joey to be wrapped in? Everyone give Mom space. She'll let us know when she's said her goodbye."

"When can we say goodbye?" Lucy asked.

"Soon, lass. Soon," he said. "A mother losing her child is a heavy, heavy blow. It will be hard on all of us. Let's stick together. I imagine we will need to give Joey a bath and dress him in something nice. That will be a good time for you all to say goodbye."

John noticed Fred making eye contact with everyone it seemed except him.

"Clete, help out with Lee and stay out of Mom's way. She may be less agreeable . . . or she may put Joey down and pick one of you up to squeeze for the week. Don't fight it. Let it happen. If you have to piss, hold it. Let someone know, and we'll figure it out. Let's be patient with her."

"John," he said, cornering him head-on. "I need your help bringing the box in and rearranging the furniture. I imagine we'll put him up on the desk; and when word gets out, folks will be coming to visit and pay respects. We need space for all of them. Do you remember when Uncle Edd died and how he was displayed in their front room?"

"Yes, sir," John said. "I remember."

"That's what we want for Joey," he said. "Mom may make some changes, but we'll do what we can to lessen her load."

"Now, I ain't never seen her this way, and I'm not sure what to expect. But if I know your mother, she'll come flying out of this like a tornado. Let's not get hit by surprise when she does. Whatever you need tomorrow, ask me; if I'm not handy, it ain't important. Any questions?" he asked.

Silence.

"Get to bed," he said.

The downhearted scattered to their posts and lay in their beds wide-eyed, listening to their mother's prayers, her anquish, her silence and woe. None of them slept. All of them cried. Lee became scared by all the distress and clung to Elaine.

Fred pulled a chair up to the bedroom door. He rested his head on the closed door and clasped his fingers together.

The sun had barely hit its stride in the morning when a solitary pony trotted up the road. His horse slowed to a walk, and the collared man slid off the side in one motion. He threw the reins around the rack near the front gate and reached back to his saddlebag, retrieving a thick black book with an ornate gold cross etched onto the leather cover.

Fred met him in the yard. The house was already buzzing with children dusting, scrubbing, moving, and turning their home into a funeral parlor.

"Morning, Fred," Father Kellen said.

"Thanks for coming, Father," said Fred.

"How is Marie?" he asked.

"'Bout how you'd expect, I guess. She's holed up in the bedroom," Fred answered.

"And the children?" he asked.

"Busy. They're keeping busy. I imagine it ain't hit home to 'em yet," he said. "Would you like to come in?"

"Let's pray first," said Father Kellen.

"All due respect, Father," Fred said. "I ain't in the mood."

The sound of a car approached the house. Both men looked. Father Kellen's horse danced around the pole, tail swatting . . . uncertain if it was in harm's way.

The vehicle passed and parked in the yard near the men.

Doc Stone stepped out, placed a hat on his head, and opened the back door for his medical bag. Closing the door, he looked at the men, smiling at first, then adjusting his countenance to match the mood.

"I'm so sorry, Fred. I hate to hear about that baby," he said. "If there is anything I can do, just let me know."

"Thank you, Doc," he said, gesturing to Father Kellen. "I believe it's between the Father and the Lord now."

"Was the baby acting ill or unusual yesterday?" Doc asked.

"Nah. He was a happy little feller. Liked to chew on Marie's apron. Didn't have enough teeth yet to smile the way he did."

"Okay," Doc said. "I've found that having a plan eases these situations with the mother. Father, will you focus on Marie immediately, and I'll examine Joey. Sometimes they don't like me poking around their baby. If you can keep her busy and facing away from me, it may be less painful for her."

39

"Blessed are those who mourn, for they shall be comforted," Father Kellen said.

"Good," Doc answered, uncertain if his response was appropriate. "I may have more questions for you, Fred, once I see him. May I?"

The trio approached the house to find five crest fallen children gazing out the front window. Fred looked official with these men, even if he wore a working man's clothes. His pressed pants and blue shirt looked sharp against the doc's suit and the father's getup. He cleaned up well, but his expression looked barren and his eyes, exhausted.

Their shoes shook like thunder down the hall toward the bedroom door.

Fred rapped on the door with a gentle hand. "Marie . . . Father Kellen and Doc Stone are here to see you and Joey . . . We're coming in . . ."

Fred reached for the knob; but before he could grip it, the door fell open to a cavernous room. Fred held an arm out gesturing the men in.

Father Kellen spoke first, "Marie . . . my child. Your grief consumes you . . ." He put an arm around her and ushered her to the bed, sitting with her facing the window and away from where Joey lie on the quilt.

Doc went about his business unwrapping the baby and placing a stethoscope on Joey's small doll-like chest. Hearing nothing, he examined the limbs, the skin, and the scalp. There was a dab of blood in one nostril, but otherwise he looked like a perfectly healthy, albeit dead, child. He found no evidence of abuse or maltreatment. He estimated the time of death to be about fifteen hours prior: 5:00 p.m., on June 1, 1928. He covered Joey with the blanket and stepped into the kitchen.

"I've never been able to do that swaddle thing with the blanket," he said to Fred. "Can you do that? Otherwise, my exam is done, and I'm sorry. My wife and I offer our sympathies to your family, Fred. You're good people. This is the last thing you deserve."

"Thanks, Doc," Fred said. "I'll let Marie know, and I'll have one of the girls wrap him. I can't do it right either. Marie is always redoing it. Must be a woman thing."

"Well, I appreciate it," Doc said. "Anything you need, Fred."

They shook hands, and Doc started.

"Oh, and give this to Marie," he said, reaching into his bag for a small brown corked bottle. "Not too much, but a little will help her sleep. The kids don't need it. If you want a swig, I'll leave that up to you."

"Thanks again," Fred said. "I'll get it to her."

Doc tipped his hat to the kids as he passed through the front room. His car roared to life and bounded back toward the main road.

Fred entered. "Back to it," he said. "Angela, can you please wrap Joey up?"

"Yes, sir," she said and sped to the bedroom.

She carefully situated Joey on the blanket, covered and tucked and wrapped. It was so much easier when he was still. She felt guilty thinking about it like that.

She lay him back on the quilt, and Father Kellen's voice rang out to the Lord, "His compassions never fail. They are new every morning. Great is your faithfulness."

He shooed Angela out, and she closed the door on her way.

It must have been an hour or two before Father Kellen came out to the porch. Fred thought he looked red-faced and sweaty. "He must have done a number on the praying," he said to John.

"Thank you, Father," Fred said, rising from the porch chair. "Marie and I certainly appreciate your prayers."

"You have a righteous woman in there, Fred McCloud," he said. "She is a blessing. You take care of her. You let me know when you want to have a burial, and I'll make myself available."

"It's appreciated," Fred said. "I had John feed and water your horse. We put him in the barn so he wouldn't have to stand out in the sun all this time."

John ran to fetch the animal.

"He's a beauty," Fred said. "John would love to have a riding horse like that, but we can only afford to have workin' horses."

"He gets me where I'm going," Father said.

John approached with the horse. "I brushed him some, too, Father," John said.

"Thank you, son," Father responded. "I'm sorry for your loss, too, boy. Death ain't easy for anyone, no matter what the age."

"Thank you, sir," John said.

Father handed his book to John and mounted the horse while John placed the Word back in his saddlebag.

"Let me know, Fred," Father Kellen said, kicking his heels back into the slick flanks of his horse.

Dust rose as the white horse rambled down the lane bouncing the good book and its shepherd into a panic. John saw Father finally pull up on the reins to bring it back in line.

"He may need to change those pants when he gets home," Fred said.

John laughed out loud.

Fred turned toward the house and took up his post on the porch, leaning forward in his chair and covering his face with his hands.

The tornado hit without warning. Flying out of the bedroom at midday, Marie ordered the girls out of her kitchen. Clete, who was assigned messenger duties, ran to the shop, where Fred and John were fitting a lid on the completed box.

"She's back," Clete spat.

Without a word, Fred bolted for the house. John swept Clete out of the way and followed. Clete, still trying to catch his breath, turned to catch up.

Approaching the house, Fred found the three girls loitering off the porch uncertain of their next move.

Marie stormed out the front door, screen door rattling on the hinge.

Surprised, everyone turned to face her fury.

"We have a lot to do for little Joey," she announced. "Girls, the Christening gown is in the hope chest. Find it, wash it, and make sure it is spotless. I want that child shining when he meets his Lord. Understand?" she said.

"Yes, Mama," they said.

"Then, I want you to bring some water for bathing him into the kitchen. Then, clean the house. Dust every corner. Nary a spider will call this house home. Understand?" she said.

"Yes, Mama," they said.

"Clete, take Lee to the barn and keep him out of the way for now," she said. "You STAY IN THE BARN. Come in at dinner time if no one has come for you yet," she said. "Understand?"

"Yes, Mama," he said.

"John, we're going to do some rearranging in the front room. Whatever you were doing can wait," she said.

She shot Fred a look that couldn't easily be defined. Anger? Sorrow? Desperation? Blame?

"Be off," she said and turned like a wounded deer, pausing before gathering strength and disappearing into the darkness.

Noticeably, Fred was left out of the work brigade.

Everyone scattered about their business. Fred stood like a wolf in a trap. He knew the only way out of this was gonna hurt.

Word spread across the hills, and in came cut chickens, cakes, and canned goods.

As Fred predicted, Mom continued to spiral. She flew out of the burial wielding dish rags, garden hoes, and chores of all kinds. Joey was buried and given to his Lord and savior. No one spoke of him, but no one forgot about him, except little Lee, who was too little to have many memories of him.

Things were different after Joey. Fred's highs were higher; his lows were lower. Mom was more child-centered than Dad-centered, and the playfulness between the pair ran off with the spoon. For Fred, he didn't sing, tease, or tickle anymore. He was always around but never anywhere to be found. John became more man than boy that year. He began handling more of the chores and missing more school. In addition, the equipment began disappearing. John couldn't figure out how or why, and so he began securing the more valuable tools with chains.

It was a lot for a ten-year-old boy to handle: 720 acres consisting of 165 acres of hay and crops and the rest in range land. Some of it rented to a neighbor, Ray Johnson, for cattle. Fred charged him by the head, and it always seemed there were more heads in the field than in the bank. John suspected there was some type of bartering involved but could never prove it. Things were getting tough in the valley.

In October 1929 it officially became tough all over, when the stock market crashed.

8

My arms and hands have been made strong . . .
Genesis 49:24

John was determined to track down the family's farm equipment that had wandered off the property

"Mom, I can do something with this place," John said. "All I need is a plow, a corn lister, a disc, and a harrow. Fred knows where it is . . . I just have to go get it."

"John, how do you plan on getting it here?" she said. "What about your school work?"

"I don't go to school much anyway," John said. "Lots of boys quit in the eighth grade. Please, Mama. Let me try."

Marie knew full well her son had inherited her stubbornness and that there would be no talking him out of it. And the boy was right . . . the family needed to increase its crops or do something different.

"Fine," she said. "But wherever you find these items, you keep your temper, John Frances McCloud. I'm not picking buckshot out of your backside, and you know we need you."

"Need him?" Fred said. "What for? Can't even make it to school."

Marie inhaled a seething breath.

"Fred, I need to find the plow. Do you remember who borrowed it," John asked.

"What do you need that for," he said.

"To plow," John said.

"Oh, well, I think Uncle Bob has it."

45

John ran down the hall toward the front door.

"Be home for dinner, John," Marie hollered.

Fred stood leaning against a kitchen chair, "Do you still pray for me, Marie?"

"I do, Fred. Every day. Every day, I pray for you," she said.

She placed the palm of her hand on his cheek, and he tilted his head into it. "I have clothes to get off the line," she said and turned as if she may never come back. Fred wanted to cry but couldn't. He hadn't even cried when they buried Joey.

A tear pooled around Fred's eye, and he savored it, unsure when another may fall. He stood in the kitchen scared and hopeless, feeling as if he had lost his family. He just didn't know where to find the strength to wake up each day without the sting of sorrow to rouse him. He wandered toward the closed bedroom door, placing a hand on it and tilting his head forward.

⤞═◉ ◉═⤛

John arrived at Uncle Bob's with Clete and Lee in tow. They brought the draft horses, Big and Shorty, and a wagon. When Uncle Bob opened the door and gave them a once over, John realized what a motley crew they were.

"What are you kids doin' here?" he asked.

"We're here to pick up the plow you borrowed from Fred," said John.

"Oh, sonny, that's all wore out. It's under those trees out yonder," he said.

"Thank you, sir," said John. "We'll get to loading it up and be out of your way."

"The three of you are going to load a plow . . . onto a wagon . . . to take home?" he asked.

"Yes, sir," said John.

"Wait here," he said, closing the door.

In a few minutes, Uncle Bob returned with boots and hat on. "I'll go down with ya'. Let's walk this way so I can holler at your cousins," he said.

The crew of misfits crossed the yard, and Uncle Bob stepped up on a fence, balanced, and placed a finger from each hand in his mouth. He whistled the strongest, clearest whistle the boys had ever heard. Bob paused. The boys looked out over what seemed to be an empty pasture.

One by one, hats appeared bouncing out of the buffalo grass. The hats became boys and men—cousins and some hired hands. "Let's go help these kids load up Fred's old plow," Bob said.

The request was met with tilted heads and curious faces, but no one raised any objections. In all, there were eight pairs of hands (three below the age of thirteen). It took the rest of the afternoon to load it. Big and Shorty were getting impatient with the process, having eaten all the grass within reach of their post. The trees were cut back; the weeds, cut out; and then parts of the plow had to be unburied.

Uncle Bob patted John on the back once the deed was done and said, "I don't know what you're gonna do with it, but best of luck."

John was tempted to brag about his plans but thought better of it. After all, if he can't get the plow to work, he's already out of business.

"Thank you, sir," he said. "I do appreciate your help." John extended his hand to shake Uncle Bob's, and he couldn't recall feeling so happy. He had sweat on his brow, his hands were dirty, and he was exhausted. This is how a man should live.

John cracked the reins on Big and Shorty a bit sharper than they were accustomed to, and they surged forward, throwing Clete and Lee into the equipment. Lee hit his head on the dull blade and got a haircut, but Clete convinced him he needed one anyway.

A chill was in the air by the time the boys pulled into the homeplace yard. The lantern was glowing in the window, and John wondered if they would be in trouble for being late or be fattened up like heroes for a job well done. It didn't matter to him, although he had worked up an appetite.

He parked the wagon near the barn and lifted Clete and Lee down to the ground.

"We did some good work today," John said. "We're going to sleep well tonight."

"I'm hungry," said Clete.

"Do you think Mama will like my haircut?" asked Lee.

"Let's go see," said John.

The trio ran toward the house.

"Welcome home, boys," the girls sang.

Fred was asleep in his chair. The warriors walked down the hall toward the kitchen, uncertain of their fate. Lye soap or prime rib? What's it gonna be?

Well, it wasn't prime rib but a pork chop that tasted better than anything they had eaten in weeks. The kids shoveled their plates empty. Lee was the first to describe their afternoon, starting with his hair cut.

"It'll do," Mom said. "Maybe I can even it out tomorrow."

Clete told about the hats walking out of the field and how strong everyone seemed to be when working together. He described the weeds and the branches as if they'd retrieved the plow from the Amazon jungle.

John sat soaking in pride; and when Mom circled the table and paused behind him to lean in for a shoulder hug and a "Thank you," he thought he might tear up like a girl.

"I better go put the horses in," he said. "May I be excused?"

"Yes, John, take Elaine and Lucy with you for help," she said. "Then you plan on cleaning up. These two are gonna get started right now."

She shooed Clete and Lee from their seats back toward the washroom.

"Spotless," she said to them, closing the door on their dusty, drooping faces.

"Yes, ma'am" said Clete.

The faucet turned on, and Clete announced, "I get to go first."

"Fine," said Lee, who sat down on the floor, feeling the back of his head and trying to imagine what his hair might look like from the back.

Clete stripped and scrubbed every part he could think of. He did a few parts twice just to be sure. He threw the wash rag at Lee, and it fell down his shoulder to the floor. Lee lay unaware of anything but his dreams.

Clete left him sleeping in the bathroom and interrupted his mom's reading of the book of Philippians, "Finally, brothers and sisters, whatever is true, whatever is noble, whatever is right, whatever is pure, whatever is lovely, whatever is admirable—if anything is excellent or praiseworthy—think about such things."

"Mom, Lee is asleep dirty on the washroom floor," he said. "What should I do?"

Marie smiled, "Let him sleep, Clete. I'll get him when we're done reading. Go get your sleep clothes on and get to bed. I'll come kiss you when I can."

"Yes, ma'am," he said. "Good night."

"Good night, Clete," she said. "Thank you for your hard work today."

"You're welcome," he said, smiling.

John and the girls entered, and Elaine and Lucy took their places near Angela for the reading. John went to the washroom to find Lee asleep, legs splayed, mouth open and snoring on the floor.

Chuckling, he went about his business of scrubbing and, when finished, stood perplexed at this quandary. Mom wants him clean, but I get in trouble when I wake people up? Deciding the safe bet was to ask Marie, he left the washroom to seek advice. He met Fred in the kitchen.

"So you got the plow okay?" Fred said.

"Yep," John said. "Uncle Bob helped us."

"Good," Fred said. "Good work, John. We better get to cleaning it up tomorrow."

"Yes, sir," John said. "Good night."

John walked past Fred without waiting for a response. He met Marie in the hall and presented Lee's dilemma.

"I'm aware, John. I'll handle it. You go to bed," she said, kissing his forehead.

"Okay, good night, Mom," he said.

She brushed her hand through John's hair, "Glad to see Lee's hair is the only casualty."

John smiled as he rounded the corner to climb the stairs.

Marie passed Fred in the bedroom and lifted Lee from the floor. Cradling him, she crept down the hallway and approached the stairs. Fred tapped her shoulder, "I can take him up."

"No Fred," she said.

Marie paused, whispering, "Fred, the world is falling apart around us, and the ground is drying up . . . killing crops and cattle like a vulture's buffet. Your son is trying to feed this family because you think we can live on air. We are not fine."

"I'm sorry, Marie," he said.

"Jesus needed help carrying his cross. Why do you think you can do it alone?" she asked. "Tomorrow is a new day. Treat it like one."

She ascended three steps and paused, "Good night, Fred."

"Good night, Marie," he said.

He listened to her steps reach the landing and open the bedroom door. He heard her pull back the sheets and place Lee down. She covered him, dropped to her knees, and said, "Okay, everyone, we have much to be thankful for tonight. Let's pray."

The group recited, "Hail, Holy Queen, Mother of Mercy, our life, our sweetness, and our hope, to thee do we cry, we poor banished children of Eve. To thee do we send up our sighs, mourning and weeping in this vale of tears. Turn then, most gracious advocate, thine eyes of mercy toward us. And after this, our exile, we pray, oh sweet Virgin Mary, that with your help we may, one day, be found worthy to see the face of God."

"And to whom do we pray?" Mom said.

"Our Father, who art in heaven, hallowed be thy name. Thy kingdom come, thy will be done, now as it is in heaven. Give us this day our daily bread and forgive us our trespasses as we forgive those who trespass against us. And lead us not into temptation, but deliver us from evil. Amen."

Fred turned and exited. The screen bounced. He stepped from the porch and withdrew into the darkness.

— 9 —

May the favor of the Lord our God rest on us;
establish the work of our hands for us.
Yes, establish the work of our hands.

Psalm 90:17

John woke early. In fact, he barely slept. Just before sunrise, he began to hear metal clanking and horses chattering, and it put the fear in him. He sprinted into his clothes and fell out the bedroom door, whizzing past his mother, who was roaming the hall.

"Where are you off to?" she asked.

"Fred's up to something," he said.

He flew out of the house, looking like a half-dressed beggar, without touching a stair. He stopped dead in his tracks as he approached the plow and wagon.

"Morning, John," Fred said. Poking his head up from the wagon bed. "You're up early."

"I heard the horses," John said, staring blankly at the once wrecked plow. "It's clean, Fred. Did you do this?"

"I couldn't sleep, so I tightened the bolts, sharpened the blade, and shined it up a bit. We've got some rust to contend with and a bent wheel, but I think we can still get the oats in by March 15," he said. "Are you up for it?"

Stumbling over himself to find the words, John simply said, "Sure."

"Good," Fred said. "Go get some breakfast, get your clothes on, and meet me at the shop. I'm gonna hitch it up and try to remove this wheel. We'll need to pound it out if we're going to plant a straight row."

"Did you eat already?" John asked.

"I'm good, John," he said. "We're working today, so don't you leave a scrap."

John hadn't felt this excited about working with Fred in a donkey's year. He couldn't describe what he felt: shocked, stunned, joyful—all of it and then some. He turned to meet his mother's gaze from the porch. She was wrapped in her housecoat and barefoot. John could see it in her eyes too . . . she was speechless.

"Come on, John," Mom said. "I'll get you some eggs and bacon." She looked out at Fred with smiling eyes. Fred tipped his head her way and hopped out of the wagon bed. He reached for Big and began leading him to the wagon neck for hitching. Shorty snorted in anticipation.

Mom followed John in the house and said, "You see, John; you lit a fire under him. Let's hope it doesn't burn out."

John beamed and sat jittery as the eggs leisurely scrambled in the pan.

John dove into his plate before it hit the table, and Mom pulled it back, leaving him drooling.

"Grace, John," she said. "We say grace and give thanks."

Reluctantly he prayed.

"Thank you heavenly Father for these eggs, bacon, and the plow. Amen," he said.

"And who was up all night working on that plow?" she added.

"And thank you for Fred working on the plow," John huffed. "Amen."

She sat the plate down and watched John inhale the food. "May I be excused?" he asked.

"Drink your milk," she said.

John reached for the glass and chugged it down as he'd seen threshers gulp water.

"Go," she said. "Have a good day."

He pushed the chair back from the table, knocking it over to the floor. He turned to pick up the chair, and his unbuttoned shirt flew into the glass on the table, pushing it near the edge.

Mom reached for the glass, steadied it, and said, "Go."

He heard her pick up the chair, scoot it under the tabletop, and laugh all the way to the sink.

In front of the shop, Big and Shorty were standing proudly with their precious cargo. The horses' breath clouded in the chilly morning air in excitement. The sun was full up, and the air was starting to lose its bite. John could hear the clang of metal on metal as Fred hammered on the dented wheel.

As he opened the shop door, Fred turned and said, "Just in time. I think it's turning out real nice."

John looked at the wheel, and it was better. He could see that one of the traction buttons had come off, but he thought that would be easy to reattach.

The morning flew by in sweat, effort, and dreaming. John caught himself imagining a good crop, food aplenty, and rain. What he found when they arrived at the field to cut soil was more like a nightmare. Russian thistles were everywhere. John guessed they averaged about three feet in diameter. A bunch of them had broken loose and were rolling by.

Fred and John stood assessing the situation.

"We'll unload the plow, and I'll get started," Fred said. "You load up as many of those thistles as you can get in the wagon, and we'll chop 'em up for the cattle to eat."

"They won't eat those dry, prickly things," John scoffed. "Let's just burn 'em."

"John, if we light those up, the wind will catch and the whole world will burn down. It's too dry," Fred said. "The cattle won't like it, but what else do they have right now? If they're hungry, they'll eat it."

"Fine," John said, thinking it was a dirty trick at the cattle's expense. "You'll be the one picking thorns outta their mouths."

"Are we gonna start up already, John?" Fred said. "We have work to do. Get to it."

John hopped off the wagon and walked to the back end. He climbed up into the bed and waited for Fred to get in position to grab the other end of the plow. With great effort and remarkable will, the two of them got the plow down.

Fred reached for Big's reins, unhitched him, and positioned him in front of the plow.

John, miffed, strode toward the biggest pile of thistles, shaking his head and arguing with his dad in his mind about feeding the cattle thorns.

Their anger dripped out of them as they labored in the hot, dry sun. After a few hours they shared a quiet wagon ride home as supper time neared. The breeze created by the moving wagon was a blessing. Big and Shorty seemed a bit resentful that their owners were relaxing while they still worked pulling the wagon home.

As they approached the homestead, Fred pulled the reins up on the horses. They stopped and Fred turned to John.

"We don't always see eye to eye, John, but you need to hear that I'm proud of you for what you did yesterday and today. You're getting to be a man now, and you see things differently than a boy does. I respect that. But I expect you to remember who your father is. I don't ask you to like me, but I ask you to respect me . . . even when I don't always deserve it," he said. "Do you hear me?"

"Yes, sir," said John. "I hear you."

"You worked hard today and I'm grateful," said Fred.

John felt shame creeping up on him. "You worked hard today too," he said. "I'm grateful."

"Now let's toss these thistles in the shuck," Fred said. "Cattle breath is not something I'm in the mood to partake of, and if picking thorns out is all up to me . . . I'd rather give the birds some shelter."

John smiled, "Thanks, Fred."

The men spread the thistles throughout the shuck and weighted them down with some dirt.

"Let's go eat," Fred said.

"Yes, sir," said John.

Fred snapped the reigns, and Big and Shorty bounded for home with renewed energy.

Upon arrival in the yard, man and beast could smell fried chicken rising from the house. Everyone but the chickens were drawn in, mouths watering. Lucy and Elaine ran down to the wagon.

"Hi, Dad. Hi, John," they said.

"Hi, girls," said Fred.

"Mom wants us to put the horses in while you boys eat," Elaine said.

"Hot damn," John said.

"As your father, I suggest you express yourself with cleaner words. As your coworker, I say well spoken," said Fred.

He put his dirt-covered hand on John's filthy shoulder, and they followed their noses up to the house. As they approached the door, they met Marie. "I'll not have filthy fingers touching my chicken," she said through the screen. "You clean up and then you can eat."

"Awww, Mom," John moaned.

"Listen to your mother," Fred said. "You go first."

John ran past Marie toward the washroom.

Lee ran up to Fred and leapt into his arms, "Daddy . . ."

"Hey, boy," he said. "How was your day? Did you keep your mama out of trouble?"

"I did," he said.

"That's a good boy," Fred said, putting him down. Clete sped over and grabbed Fred's pant leg.

"Dad, Dad . . . I found thirteen eggs today," he beamed.

"Good job, Clete," he said. "Did you break any?"

"Only one," he said.

"Well, I bet your mama didn't need that one, did she?" he said.

"That's what I told her," Clete said.

Mom shooed the boys back into the house.

"It's good to see you again, Fred," she said.

"It's good to be back," he said.

"Are you feeling okay?" she asked.

"Tired and hungry . . . just how you like me," Fred said.

She smiled, "Come in; John will be done any second. I made you your favorite."

"Thanks, Marie, I appreciate it," he said. "I don't suppose, if your chicken is off limits, I can give you a hug?"

"One won't hurt," she said.

They held each other close, and she missed the feel of him, the warmth of him. The smell of him she could do without but knew it was the result of a hard day's work, which they all needed from him. She felt a tremble in his shoulder.

"Are you okay?" she said, pushing him back. "I felt a shaking. Are you seizing?"

She looked determinedly in each of his eyes. She couldn't tell if he were pale through the dirt and sunburn.

"Marie, I'm fine," he assured her. "I worked hard today. My body didn't enjoy it as much as you and John did. I'm not a young buck anymore you know."

John ran half-baked to the table and shoved a chicken leg into his mouth. He closed his eyes as the taste melted on his tongue.

Fred walked toward the washroom. "Is it good?" he asked.

"Fred . . . it's the best," John said.

"Well, leave some for me," Fred said.

Fred reached for the doorknob on the washroom and felt his hand twitch. His fingers began to tighten up and feel painful. He closed his eyes dreading this . . . knowing it was coming and certain Marie would be wrecked with worry. He knew he wouldn't have time to hide this one from the family. He reached out with his other hand, gripped the door, and turned the knob. He moved into the washroom and pulled the door closed . . . staggering to lock it. His knee gave out and down he went. He stiffened up and began thrashing, kicking the door of the washroom. The convulsions seemed harsher than he'd had in the past, although he wasn't entirely aware of reality. His head hit the bathtub more than once, and he cried out without wanting to.

He could hear someone pounding on the door and Marie's voice, "Fred . . . Fred. . . . Stay with me, Fred . . ."

Grateful he got the door locked, Fred was glad Marie wouldn't see him this way again. Fearful that he got the door locked, he wondered if this might be the one to take him home.

He tried to focus on Marie's voice . . . "Fred . . . Fred . . . Stay with me, Fred . . ."

Blackness came on him first and then silence.

10

Have mercy on me, O Lord, for I am weak;
Heal me, for my bones are troubled.
Psalm 6:2

Marie lay down in front of the locked washroom door and leveled her eyes through the gap above the threshold and below the door.

"Fred," she said. "I'm calling Doc Stone. You hold on to the bathtub leg if you can. We'll get to you."

Fred's spasms were slowing but seemed to be consistent in degree. The sound of his boots hitting the wall echoed throughout the house. Marie rose to a crowd of alarmed sons and daughters. The children had never witnessed one of Fred's seizures, as he was usually pretty good about sensing their arrival and hid himself away until they passed.

Marie reached for the phone, "Doc Stone please. It's an emergency."

Moving her mouth away from the mouthpiece, she said, "John, we have to figure a way in there."

John bolted out of the house toward the shop. He grabbed the hammer Fred used to reshape the plow wheel and ran back to the house, leaping the stairs and tearing the screen door off one hinge. He grabbed a knife on the way past his plate and pushed his way through the pint-size audience. He placed the knife below the door hinge bolt and hammered it up and through the casing. He caught his thumb once but tried not to curse, unsuccessfully. "Shit," he said, moving quickly down to the second hinge. Mom finished on the phone and dropped it rather than hanging it up.

John repeated the task, and Mom ripped the door open as John finished the third hinge bolt. Just before it would have beaned Clete on the head, John caught the falling door and drug it over to the wall.

Mom embraced Fred's head in her lap, which served as a buffer to keep him from hitting the tub.

"John," she said. "Hold his legs."

"Kids," she commanded. "To the porch. He wouldn't want you to see him this way."

Before herding the onlookers out the precariously hanging screen door, Angela handed her mom a cool, wet washcloth, which she placed on his forehead.

Like waiting for the last popcorn kernel to pop, the makeshift medics waited for Fred's body to be still. He was unconscious; and by the time his muscles relaxed, John removed both boots and Marie unbuttoned his shirt. She used the washcloth to wipe away sweat and dirt and spittle, which clung to the corners of Fred's mouth.

Marie said, "John, your daddy just can't work a full day with this illness."

"Grandma Alise says it's a demon," John said.

"Well, Grandma Alise doesn't know a mule from a mirror. It's a disease. The doctors haven't figured it out yet. They will someday . . . you just watch," she said. "You'll see."

"Yes, ma'am," said John. "Will he wake up?"

"It will take a while. He wore himself out twitching the way he does . . . and on top of being up all night and working all day. Poor man. Do you think we can carry him to bed?"

"I think so," said John. "You take his legs, and I'll grab his shoulders."

Marie lay Fred's head down on the floor and negotiated the little walking space around Fred's gnarled body. John let her exit the room completely and then took his place by Fred's face. Marie reached down, knelt, and wedged one of Fred's shins around each of her hips. John hooked his arms underneath Fred's arm pits.

"On the count of three," said Marie. "One . . . two . . . three."

In unison the pair lifted and balanced their load, taking slow steps toward the bedroom. Marie kicked Fred's boots out of the way and paused at the bedside. John entered on cue with the rest of Fred and aligned himself against the length of the bed.

"I'll set his legs down first and then pull the covers back," she said.

"Okay," said John, starting to feel the weight of Fred's body.

Marie placed Fred's legs on the quilt one at a time and ran around the bed to grab at the covers. She jerked them down the length of the bed, and John leaned forward with Fred's body, placing him on a pillow facing the window. He worked to free his arm from beneath the weight of Fred's shoulder.

"Thank you, John," she said. "Will you send Angela in with a basin of water and a cloth? You can go finish your meal."

"Okay," said John. "Let me know if you need anything else." John glanced at his father, who seemed pale. There was blood dripping from a cut on his head, and he couldn't help but think of Joey. He turned to complete his duty and hollered down the hall for Angela.

"Mom wants you to take in a wash rag and a basin of water," said John. "Everyone else can come in if you want. Dad's in bed."

"Is he okay?" asked Elaine.

"I think so," said John. "Doc Stone will know."

John returned to a plate of cold fried chicken and decided that it was still the best chicken he'd ever eaten.

Clete and Lee joined John at the table.

"How'd the plow work," asked Clete.

"Good," said John. "I'll show you later if Mom says it's okay."

"Can I come?" said Lee.

"Why not?" said John. "You have to start learning farming too you know."

Lee beamed.

"It's fun," said Clete. "You'll like it."

Lee couldn't wait to start.

"Eat your food, John," he said. "Let's go."

There was a knock at the door, "Hello? . . . Anyone here? . . . It's Doc Stone . . ."

"Come in, Doc," Angela yelled, peeking out from the bedroom.

"In here."

Doc tipped his hat at the crew as he walked through the kitchen to the bedroom. He closed the door after him, and an occasional mumble pierced the silence.

Angela exited with a basin of dirty water. She took it outside, dumped it off the porch, and refilled it with clean water.

"John," she called. "Can you fix that front door? Someone's gonna get hurt."

"When I'm done eating . . ." he said.

And that's when it hit him. Fred would be out of commission for a while, and everything would fall back on John's shoulders. A field barely turned, a crop needing to be planted, a farm on its last wheel, and no rain in sight.

John's mood took a turn for the worse. He chewed his chicken with renewed vigor and wiped a finger across his plate to get every bit of flavor from it.

Elaine and Lucy set about cleaning up the table and kitchen, and John excused himself. He picked up the hammer and knife and started toward the screen door. Upon examination he realized a chunk of wood that held the hinge was torn from the frame.

"Rotted," he said. He should replace the whole board, but finding a good piece of available wood could be challenging. He used the knife to tap the functioning hinge out and moved the door to the side of the frame so that no one had to contend with its current state.

"Angela, I'm going to the shop," he said down the hallway.

"Okay," she said.

He decided it wasn't any use to steal a good piece of wood from something else since that would leave it in a compromised position. He found some wood glue and a couple of screws that were twice as long as the ones originally used.

He returned to the house just as Doc was leaving.

"Good work helping your mother," he said.

"Thank you, sir," said John. "How is he?"

"He'll be okay," he said. "He'll have a hell of a headache for a few days and might sleep for a week, but he'll jump out of it."

"Hmm . . . that's good," said John, with just a seasoning of bitterness.

"You take care of things, John," he said. "Your mama is gonna need you."

"Yes, sir," said John. "Good night."

"Night, son," he said while sliding into his car. "Call with any questions."

"Thank you, sir," said John.

Doc Stone drove down the lane into the setting sun; and for the first time, John thought maybe he should join him as far as Anselmo and then hop a train to somewhere. California maybe. New York. Somewhere he can work without the pain in the ass of being his father's son.

He turned toward his next project and realized he had been squeezing the screws in his hand with such fervor that he was bleeding. He pulled the screw out of his palm and wiped it on his pants. He sat down in front of the door frame and called into the house, "Can I get a rag?"

Lucy trotted down the hall with a dish rag. "Here," she said.

"Thanks," said John, wrapping his hand with it. "Can you tie it," he said stretching his arm out to Lucy.

"Oh, John," she said. "You work too hard. What did you do this time?"

"Nothing," he said. "Just clumsy, I guess."

"When you're done, you better wash it and put some alcohol on it so it doesn't get infected," she said.

"Okay," he said. "I'll do that."

A chill fell over the land as John worked to glue and repair the porch door. He thought it turned out pretty good, considering. He swung it back and forth between his hands a few times and decided it was as good as it was gonna be.

He could barely keep his eyes open and took a seat in the porch chair. The sun had abandoned him, and he had finished up by moonlight. This was his favorite time of day—darkness, cicadas, buffalo grass whistling. And before he knew what hit him, he was asleep.

"John," his mother whispered, shaking his shoulder. "Get up, John.

Let's get you to bed."

He had no idea how long he had been asleep. She helped him stand up and walked him upstairs to his room. He crawled over his snoring brothers to his slice of mattress and fell, dead to the world.

He could feel his mother removing his boots. He heard her kiss her hand and felt it rest on his forehead.

"Good night, John," she said. "God bless you."

Heaviness weighed on his eyelids, and he gave up the day.

11

. . . I also labor, striving according to His energy,
which works in me mightily.

Colossians 1:29

The irregular contour of the Sandhills, the rare cedar trees, and the wide vistas of unoccupied country have an allure of their own. It is still Indian country, though the Natives have long been gone. Cutting across country, over the prairie and the shoulders of connected hills, is rough going, with a fair chance of getting at least temporarily lost. Decidedly, it is a country for horseback riding, which is a mode of transportation entirely too slow for the young or busy, of which John was both.

He cursed the wagon for its bulkiness but knew it was the only way to get oat seed back from Claude Bates's farm near Lillian. Claude was a friend to everyone; married for a short time to a woman who ran off with the wind, he now lived a bachelor's life. Each spring he gave oat seed to everyone who needed it. He only asked that the same amount be returned at harvest. It was a generous arrangement and quite risky on his part given the current drought.

"Are we there yet?" Clete asked from the wagon bed.

"Almost," said John, even though he wasn't certain.

"I'm bored," said Clete.

"Not my problem," said John.

"Why didn't we bring Lee?" said Clete.

"Because we won't have room once we pick up the seed. I only brought you for company, and I'm sorely regretting it," said John.

Clete lay back down in the wagon and began describing the shapes he saw in the clouds.

"That cloud looks like a horse," he said. "That one looks like a potato."

John couldn't help but look to see the potato-shaped cloud.

"Don't they all look like potatoes?" said John.

"You have to use your imagination," said Clete.

"I guess you're right," said John, shaking his head.

Clete laughed. The wagon rolled on toward the Bates' place, clanking Claude's praises all the way.

Fred woke feeling as if a horse had kicked him in the skull. He reached up expecting half his head to be out in the yard. Instead, he found a couple of small stitches. Confused, he looked toward the window; and although it was daylight, he felt as if he didn't know what day it was or how long he'd been in bed. His legs felt stiff . . . like they became part of the mattress. He couldn't remember having an accident. He couldn't remember a seizure. It sure didn't feel like the aftermath of a typical seizure. He strained to remember working with John and the plow and the smell of fried chicken. He wondered if anyone else was hurt.

"Marie," he said, knowing it wasn't loud enough for her to hear. "Marie," he tried again, feeling his head pound out each syllable. His voice, barely recognizable to himself, sounded as if God took a wood plane from the shop and thinned his throat down.

The door creaked open, and Angela peeked inside.

"Daddy?" she said.

"Marie?" he said.

"No, Daddy, it's me, Angela," she said. "I'll get Mama. You stay right there."

Fred closed his eyes so that the sunlight wouldn't ignite the pain in his head. The rosy brightness that filtered through his eyelids reminded him of blood.

"Fred," said Marie, rushing to his side. "Fred, honey, how are you feeling?"

"Did a horse kick me?" he asked.

"A seizure. A big one," she said.

Fred said nothing.

"Doc said you might not remember much, so don't fret about it," she said. "I'm just so glad to see you awake."

Fred smiled.

"Where's John?" Fred asked.

"He and Clete went to get oat seed from Claude Bates," she said. "He's determined to get that crop in for you."

"Not for me, Marie. For you . . . I'll never be good enough for you . . . he's got that part right anyway," he said.

"Aw, Fred, I won him over with fried chicken and mashed potatoes. And he takes after you; he just doesn't realize it yet," she said.

Fred tried to push himself up on the pillow. Marie put her hands on his shoulders to stop him.

"You're not to get outta bed until Doc Stone gives you a once over," she said. "Doctor's orders."

"Doctor schmoctor," he said.

"My orders," she said.

He lay back down.

"Can the kids come see you?" She asked. "They've been worried."

"Sure," he said. "Send 'em in."

"I'll call Doc Stone," she said.

She leaned forward and kissed him on the forehead.

"Welcome back," she said.

Fred smiled with effort. Her kiss felt warm on his skin.

She left the room without shutting the door, and in flew Angela, Lucy, Elaine, and Lee.

"Daddy, Daddy," they sang. "We missed you!"

They covered him with kisses and hugs, and he felt like a bitch with hungry puppies.

"Okay, okay, everyone. I'm glad you missed me," he said. "I have missed each and every one of your faces."

"Even me?" said Lee.

"Especially you," he said, reaching out for him and lifting him up into bed with him.

Lee beamed.

"Girls, have you been good for your mama?" he asked.

"Oh yes, Daddy. We've been working really hard and saying our prayers and checking on you every chance we could," Lucy said.

"Good girls," he said. "You are each gonna make wonderful, God-fearing wives someday."

They all blushed.

"Now, Daddy needs a little quiet time before Doc arrives," he said. "Thanks for taking good care of things."

"You're welcome, Daddy!" Elaine said.

Lee clung to Fred like a barnacle. Elaine reached forward to peel him off, and Fred stopped her.

"Lee, can you snuggle quietly with Daddy?" he asked.

"Yes, sir," said Lee.

"Then you can stay. If you get rowdy, you'll have to go out to the other room," he said.

"Okay, Daddy," he said and looked at all the exiting girls like he'd just eaten their canary.

Fred sunk deeper into the pillow, and Lee cuddled up tight.

"I missed you, Daddy," said Lee.

"I missed you, boy," said Fred. "I truly did."

Fred fell asleep, and Lee lay very still, listening to his dad's heart. Thump, thump. Thump, thump. Thump, thump. He loved the beat and wondered if everyone's heart sounded the same. Maybe each person had a special rhythm that, when played together, made beautiful music for God. He imagined the Lord listening to the world's song and decided God was pleased. It made Lee happy to be a part of it.

Marie entered the room to find Lee asleep on Fred's chest smiling. Fred looked peaceful. She set the glass of water on the end table and closed the door on her way out.

She sat in Fred's chair, gathered the remaining children together, and said, "It's time we thank God for bringing back your daddy. Let's pray . . ."

John and Clete arrived at the Bates' farm right about lunch time; Mom packed a few pieces of leftover chicken, some bread, and a jug of water. The wagon bounced into Claude's yard to find another wagon filled to the brim with seed on the way out. John didn't recognize its driver but tipped his hat to him. Clete waved. Claude Bates stood in the yard, waiting for John's approach.

"Hi there," said John.

"Hello to you," Claude said.

"I'm John McCloud. Fred's boy," he said. "He asked me to come pick up some oat seed, if you had any to spare."

"Sure thing, John," Claude said. "Nice to meet you. And who is your helper?"

"My name's Clete," Clete said.

"Not sure he's a helper just yet," said John. "He's company though."

"Where's your daddy today?" Claude asked. "Seems daring to send a young man and a little one on such a big job."

"He's ill, sir," John said.

"Hmmm . . . I'm sorry to hear that," Claude said. "Is it from the drink?"

"No, sir," he said. "Some type of seizure. Heatstroke maybe. We'd been plowing, and it happened just after."

"Well, I can't say that I'm happy to hear he's sick, but I am pleased to hear he's working," he said. "Losing that boy was hard on him. I can't imagine. Of course, it's hard for me to imagine sons at all, given that I ain't married no more; but I suppose the solo life brings its share of troubles too."

"Well, if you ask me," said John. "You got it all figured out."

"Do I?" said Claude, smiling coyly. "Well, let's get to it then."

John pulled the wagon over to the silo and pulled the tailgate down. Clete handed him a shovel and hopped out of the wagon.

"Clete," said John. "How about you hold Big and Shorty so they don't spook."

"Will do," said Clete, circling to the front and grabbing Shorty's bridal.

Claude said, "Help yourself, John. I'll be right back."

"Thank you, sir," John said.

John dug the shovel blade in deep and tried to keep it balanced all the way back to the wagon. He could see he was making little progress by the trail of seed falling to the ground. One step forward, two steps back is what his mom always said to describe those who suffered from a lack of common sense. It occurred to John that there was probably a better way to get this done but decided he wasn't prepared to try out any alternative methods. For the time being, he fit the lack-of-sense bill. He continued digging and throwing the seed back into the wagon. Claude appeared from the barn with a couple of large buckets.

He threw one down at John's feet. "Try this," he said.

Genius—John thought—this man is a genius. No woman, no kids, and buckets and seed to spare.

They worked together as the sun beat down on their foreheads. John could feel sweat rolling down his back, and he could see Claude was glistening too.

The wagon full of oat seed was a sight to behold. John handed his bucket back to Claude.

"Thank you again, sir," he said.

"Call me Claude," he said. "You tell your folks I say hello. Tell Fred I've got a hired man looking for work that I can't give him. If Fred's interested in help while he recovers, I'll send him over."

John almost peed himself with excitement. "Yes, sir. Send him over, sir," he spat.

"You'll have to negotiate a price for him," he said. "He don't work free."

"I understand, sir," John said. "Fred and he can work that out. I can promise you he won't get fat or bored."

"That sounds about right," Claude said. "I'll send him over tomorrow."

"Thank you, sir," John said, extending a dirty, sticky, grateful hand.

The men shook hands, and John felt like God had finally taken notice of his plight. What a wonderful feeling it was to imagine God, the King of Kings, showing special favor.

"I'll see you after harvest," said John.

"It's a plan. Best of luck," he said.

John and Clete loaded up in the wagon and began their journey. John was smiling from ear to ear, and Clete was half-asleep next to him. It occurred to John after a few miles that the wagon rode a lot smoother with some weight in it. Big and Shorty may have held a differing opinion, as they seemed a little crankier.

The sun was behind them, and John could feel evening coming on. As they pulled into their own yard, John could smell something cooking that he couldn't put his finger on. He saw Fred sitting on the porch chair and waved. Fred returned the gesture but didn't rise to greet them. Elaine and Lucy came out and grabbed hold of Big and Shorty.

"Go get some food, John," Elaine said. "We'll handle them."

Lucy reached up for Clete and pulled him down out of his seat.

"I got to hold the horses still," he said.

"Good for you, Clete," Lucy said. "What would John do without you?"

"Let's eat," John said. He approached the porch and paused near Fred.

"How you feeling?" John asked.

"Like a bull drug me across the canyon," Fred answered. "But grateful to be awake. Looks like you had a good day."

"Yep," John said. "Claude is a pretty nice guy."

"He is that," said Fred. "He'll have a warm spot in heaven—that's for sure."

"He says he has a hired man looking for work," said John.

Fred looked at John sideways.

"He's sending him over tomorrow," John said.

"You think we can afford him?" Fred asked.

"Don't know," John said. "I thought you should talk to him and figure that out."

Fred looked at John for a moment.

"Good work today, son," he said. "Go get some grub. Kiss your mama. She's been worried."

"Yes, sir," John said, entering the house.

Lucy and Clete followed. "Hi, Daddy!" said Clete on the way by.

"Hello, son," he said.

Fred watched Elaine lead the horses and wagon over to the barn. She entered and a lamp glow grew out of the darkness. Fred stood cautiously looking out over the yard. He listened to the clanking of silverware inside the house, the mumble of children discussing their days; and he decided maybe he needed to bite the bullet and hire a man, a good man to help John out during planting. He thought he could get back in the saddle before the guy put him in the poorhouse.

He stepped down off the porch to stretch his legs and to go try to help Elaine and Lucy. Cicadas serenaded him, and a breeze caught his nose. Smells like rain, he thought. He stopped and looked up at the clouds and felt hope spring up within him. He paused by the wagon of seed. He ran his fingers through it and smelled it.

"Smells like spring," he said.

"It sure does, Daddy," said Lucy. "And it smells like rain."

Fred looked up to the sky as if betrayed by his best friend, "Let's hope . . ."

12

You have put gladness in my heart.
Psalm 4:7

About midmorning a young man rode up the lane on a weary-looking Palomino horse. He jumped down from the saddle like a man who may have had too much to drink the night before. Fred noticed he walked through the yard at an angle but ended up approaching the porch directly in front of Fred's chair.

"Morning," he said.

"Morning," Fred said. "Can I help you?"

"Maybe," he said. "Claude Bates sent me over thinking you may have a need for a farm hand."

"Did he?" said Fred.

"Yes, sir," he said. "I'd be honored to help out if you need me. I can do about anything, and I have a knack for fixing things."

"You got a knack for breaking 'em too?" asked Fred.

The man stood perplexed, "No, sir. I'm a very cautious man."

"Hmmm . . ." Fred said. "Well, we do have a lot of things that need fixin'. You got a name?"

"Miles Sweeney," he said.

"You from around here?" Fred asked.

"No, sir. I came up from Kansas. My daddy passed on, and Mama moved to Hill City. I came here looking for work, and I send home what I can."

"What a good son," Fred said.

Miles stood silently trying to decide if Fred was being kind or sarcastic.

Marie and John came out onto the porch. Miles removed his hat. "Morning, ma'am," he said.

"Did Claude send you?" asked John.

"Yes," Miles said. "My name is Miles Sweeney."

John looked to Fred, "Have you settled on a price?"

Miles looked hopeful. Fred spit off the side of the porch. "Not yet," Fred said.

"He says he's good at fixing things," Fred said. "How 'bout we see what you can do with that lister over yonder. We can talk price once we see what we're paying for."

"Fair enough, sir," said Miles.

John leapt down from the porch, extending a hand to Miles. "Let me show it to you," he said.

The two young men walked toward the shop, where the tools and the lister were residing.

Marie turned to Fred, "Thank you, Fred. You won't regret it. At least not if he's a good worker."

. "I think he is. His hands are rough, and the sun has colored his skin around the eyes," said Fred. "You know a man is a hard worker when he gets the white whiskers from squinting in the sun. I think he'll work out just fine."

Marie was impressed at Fred's observation. She smiled at him and extended a hand to his shoulder.

"You really are a good man, Fred," she said.

"Well, I'm a real son of a bitch too," he said with a fiery voice.

"Are you upset with me?" Marie asked.

"No," Fred said apologetically. "Just tired of my body giving up on me, my head spinning around, and my son treating me like a spent dairy cow."

"Oh, Fred," she said. "You know John means well. As he grows up, life will start adding up for him. He'll see you did what you could, when you could . . . You remember what you were like at his age?"

"Yeah," Fred said. "Respectful."

Marie's head drooped forward. Fred stepped off the porch and moved toward the barn.

"I'm going to check on the milk cows," he said.

Marie watched him walk toward the barn dragging his soul through the dirt behind him.

Noise started emerging from the shop. Marie sat in the porch chair, uncertain of what she could do . . . so she bowed her head and prayed.

"Father God, there's no use in me explaining this to you, because you are all knowing. Please give me some wisdom that will help me bring John and Fred to a point of kindness. I know you have plans for both of them, and I want your will to be done. Just press on my heart what I should say to each of them to get them working together and not against each other. Thank you, Lord,"

She raised her head to find John standing in front of her at the porch railing.

"Good luck with that," John said.

"Oh, John," Marie said. "Can't you see your father is suffering?"

John tugged at his ear. "Where'd the old man go?" John asked.

"To check on the milk cows," she said.

"Go talk to him," she said. "Nicely. Tell him what you think of Miles and what you think we should pay him. Thank him for considering it."

"Isn't it punishment enough to have to do all the work around here?" asked John.

"John Francis McCloud . . . you just escorted a hardworking young man who is gonna be helping you. Are you still complaining? You aren't too old for lye soap you know."

"Fine," said John. "I'll do the best I can."

"Do better than that," Marie said. "God has always answered my prayers one way or another, and you had better prepare yourself for his answer to today's prayer. Either God's grace or your mama's frying pan are gonna hit you like a brick."

"Yes, Mama," said John.

John moved to the barn as though he were kicking the remains of Fred's soul through the yard in front of him.

A farm fuel hauler out of Anselmo parked down the lane just in view of the yard. The driver stepped out and lifted the hood, and steam rose up from the engine. The man kicked the dirt and circled in front of the vehicle, displaying a lot of passion and an impressive vocabulary.

"He must've overheated," said John. "I have to milk. Why don't you take a bucket of water down to him."

"Okay," said Clete. "Lee, let's go."

The two boys obtained a milk bucket from the barn and ran over to the well. After filling it with cool, clear water, each child grabbed a side of the wire bucket handle and carried it slowly down the lane toward the stranded fellow.

They met the man on the way.

"Hello there," the man said.

"Need some water?" asked Lee.

"That is exactly what I need," he said.

"Lucky we saw you," said Clete.

"You boys just made my day," he said. "Can I help you with that?"

He reached forward and grabbed the wire handle in the center. The boys released their holds and looked up at him.

"My name's Clete," Clete said.

"I'm Lee," said Lee.

"Pleased to meet you boys," he said. "My name is Charlie. Charlie Mohat."

"Can we help you put the water in?" Clete asked.

"It's pretty hot right now," he said. "Why don't you come down and keep me company."

"Okay," Clete said.

Lee and Clete raced down toward his truck and marveled at the size of it. After examining the vehicle with interest and respect, they found a seat on the road in front of the truck's radiator.

Charlie removed the cap, using a dirty rag from his back pocket. He poured the water into the radiator, and the boys listened to the "Chhhhhhhh" sound of the coolness hitting the metal.

"Chhhhhhh," Clete said.

"Chhhhh," Lee said.

Charlie laughed at the pair of them.

"You are some pretty cute kids," he said. "I tell you what—as a token of my gratitude, I'm gonna bring you boys a surprise this afternoon."

They gasped, looking at each other with big eyes.

"Today?" said Lee.

"Today," said Charlie. "My shift is over. As soon as I get back, I'm gonna pick up your surprise and come right back to your farm with it. How'd that be?"

"Wow," said Clete. "That sounds nice."

"I'm gonna wait right here," said Lee.

"Well now, it will be a few hours," said Charlie. "I'll be riding my horse, so don't hold your breath. But you both have my word that I will bring you a surprise late this afternoon. Now I gotta go. Thanks for your help. I will see you later."

The boys stepped out of the way, not wanting to hinder his efforts toward obtaining their surprise.

"See you later," Clete and Lee said.

The driver tousled Lee's hair and hopped in the cab.

"Today," he said, pointing a finger at the boys as he drove off.

Clete and Lee stood in amazement at the man's kindness. They watched him drive out of sight before picking up the bucket and turning back up the lane.

They ran straight to the barn, where John was milking.

"John," Clete said, "Charlie is going to bring us a surprise."

"Isn't that great?" said Lee. "I wonder what it will be."

John looked sideways at them from under the cow. "You think maybe he might bring you a kick in the ass?" he said.

Offended, they both said, "No."

"Let's go tell Lucy," said Lee, and off they ran toward the house, meeting Fred on the porch.

"Whoa, whoa," said Fred. "What's got you boys in a huff?"

Clete and Lee relayed the wonderful events of their morning, and Fred just shook his head.

"Congratulations," he said, ushering the boys into the house. "A good deed never goes unnoticed."

Fred assumed his position in the porch chair, putting his boots up on the porch railing. John approached the house carrying two buckets full of fresh milk. Cats and kittens flocked toward his path to gobble up any droplets spilling onto the ground.

"Looks good," said Fred.

John said nothing. He stepped up on the porch and set one bucket down and reached up to pull open the screen door. He held the door frame with his back and leaned forward for the second bucket. Lifting it, he balanced himself with the weight of both buckets and entered the house. A few minutes later he exited the home, spitting off the staircase onto the ground. Fred said nothing. John headed out to the barn and began preparing Angela's saddle horse Midge for a trip out to the windmill.

John mounted the horse and kicked its sides with his heels. Midge bounded out the barn door and down the lane. Fred watched his eldest son, "the Lone Ranger," as he liked to refer to him, ride toward the rye field. Fred lifted his hat and squared it over his eyes, shielding them from the sun.

A few hours passed, and Fred woke to the sound of a horse trotting up the lane. It wasn't Midge. It was someone he didn't recognize.

"Hello," the man said from atop his horse. "You must be Clete and Lee's father."

"Depends on if you got good news or bad news," said Fred.

"Good news, sir," he said. "They helped me out of a pinch this morning by bringing me water for my overheated truck. I told them I would bring them a surprise."

"Awwww," Fred said. "They were pretty excited about that. Let me get 'em for you."

"Clete . . . Lee," Fred yelled. "Your surprise is here."

"They'll be right here," said Fred, who had no idea if his sons were at the house or in the barn or on the moon.

Marie came out of the house.

"Hi," she said to the young stranger. "Can I help you?"

"Yes, ma'am," said Charlie. "Two of your sons helped me today, and I brought them a surprise as a thank you."

"I heard a little something about a big surprise," she said. "They're helping their brother on the windmill about one half mile that way."

"Thank you, ma'am," he said. "They are good boys."

"Thank you," she said. "We like them."

Following her finger north, Charlie's horse sauntered toward the windmill. As soon as the horse crested the hill, Lee saw him and came running toward him. "Clete," Lee yelled, "Clete."

Clete turned his head to see Charlie approaching and dropped the piece of wood he was holding for John.

"Great," said John. "Another interruption."

Following Lee down the hill, Clete caught up with him at the foot of Charlie's horse. Charlie had a potato sack tied around his shoulder.

He hopped down from his saddle. "I told you I would bring you something," he said.

He placed the potato sack on the ground, and Clete and Lee could hear a squeaking sound coming from a mound that was trying to find a way out of the sack.

"What is it?" asked Lee.

Charlie opened the tie at the end of the bag, and out came a German shepherd puppy. It bounded toward Clete and then hopped toward a grasshopper that caught its eye. Then the dog stuck its hind end in the air and jumped on Lee. The dog nibbled Lee's ear and covered his face with soggy kisses. Lee giggled and embraced the puppy in his arms. He fell back and let the dog jump and sniff and grab at his clothing. Clete got a pet in every now and again, but everyone there knew it was Lee who came out of the day with a new best friend.

"Thank you," said Lee, "Thank you, Charlie. I love him."

"He's a good dog. His mama was a good dog, too," he said.

"He's a beauty," said Clete. "Really . . . thank you."

"Thank you," Charlie said, extending a hand to Clete for a shake. "You give him a good home."

"We will," Clete and Lee said together.

Charlie waved to John, who was not-so-patiently waiting for his support staff to return from break. John held his hand up and acknowledged the gesture. Charlie mounted his horse and disappeared down the lane.

"What are we gonna name him?" Lee asked.

"I don't know," said Clete. "You'll know when you know."

"That's it!" said Lee. "Uno."

"Works with me," said Clete.

"Today," yelled John.

Lee and Clete returned to John at the windmill and finished the job of patching the leg brace. Uno tagged along, sniffing and peeing on every piece of wood he could find. Lee and Clete cackled with joy when the dog lifted a leg near John's boot. John gave a sharp glance toward the dog.

"It'll be a short, happy life for you if you piss on me," said John.

Uno barked and wagged his tail, jumping backward toward Lee.

Lee picked Uno up and hugged him. "We're gonna be the best of friends," he said.

Uno licked his cheek and nibbled on his shirt collar. Lee put the dog down on the ground and said, "Come on, Uno. Let's go meet Mom." Lee ran toward the house, and Uno chased him, nipping at his heels all the way.

Lee and Uno became inseparable, and at night Uno slept on Lee's feet. Clete and John, who shared a bed with Lee, complained about the arrangement until winter hit and Uno had grown big enough to provide warmth for all their feet.

One Sunday, while the family was at mass in Anselmo, Uno was accidently left in the house with a roasted turkey resting on the open oven door. Marie felt, if not for prayer, Uno would have certainly relented to his animal instincts and devoured it, leaving nothing but the wishbone. However, Uno made sure the turkey didn't move for the length of the family's trip to town. There wasn't so much as a bread crumb out of place. No one but Lee gave Uno his due credit.

— 13 —

There is no greater love than to lay down one's life for one's friends.
John 15:13 (Darby Translation)

Uno became a family member, rather than a farm dog, and the greatest foe the prairie rattlesnakes had ever seen. Fred appreciated Uno's knack for scaring salesmen away from the house. John enjoyed the distraction he provided to Clete and Lee so that he could get more work done. The girls loved Uno for his ability to give a kiss at the most inappropriate times, and they loved rubbing his belly, which Uno didn't mind either. Clete held him in the highest respect for his rattlesnake-hunting ability. Lee more than loved Uno. The dog became his confidant, his playmate, and his willing accomplice in ridding his plate of food he didn't like. Marie also admired Uno's snake-hunting skills in the summertime, but she grew to cherish him during the winter months, when the snakes were more likely to be living in shared spaces.

The dog was a natural-born rattlesnake killer. He would freeze up like a statue when he spotted his prey. He would let the rattler think he wasn't going to approach by just observing it for a few moments; then with a series of vertical bounces, he was on the snake, circling it, throwing up dust at it, tormenting it. The snake's nature was to coil into a pile and strike from the top. Uno had a way of discouraging its coil by jumping up and coming down with both front paws on a part of the snake, most commonly behind the neck. The snake usually didn't know what to do—it would attempt to recoil only to be tackled again and again. When Uno became bored with the game, he would grab it behind the head and give it a quick snap and release. Most often, the dog wasn't satisfied until the snake lay in pieces. Clete and Lee began saving the rattles left in Uno's wake, and they collected several jars within the first year.

One year into Uno's life in McCloud Valley, he was Lee's best friend. He accompanied Clete and Lee everywhere, which always comforted Marie, knowing she wouldn't lose her sons to rattlesnakes—to great ideas gone wrong perhaps, but rattlesnakes were off the danger list as long as Uno was in tow.

In early June, Clete and Lee and Uno walked out toward the windmill to check on a recent repair John had made. Clete led the way, Lee followed within fifteen feet, and Uno trotted about six feet to Lee's right, as any good wingman would. Upon arriving at the windmill, Clete and Lee went about their business making sure that everything was working properly. Uno strayed off about twenty-five feet and almost immediately assumed his statue-like position.

"There he goes again," said Clete.

"That dog is amazing," said Lee.

While the attraction of a good Uno snake fight was alluring, the boys knew John was waiting for their return before he left to go out to the field. They determined everything looked good, and Lee called for Uno, "Uno, let's go, boy."

Uno turned toward Lee, and the distraction provided an opportunity for the rattlesnake. From the sea of buffalo grass flew a writhing rope with mouth wide open; it dug its fangs into Uno's nose. The dog yelped, taking a step back and shaking its head until the snake fell to the ground.

"Oh no," said Lee. "Oh no."

"Let's get him home," said Clete.

"Come on, Uno," they rang out to him, desperately patting their legs with their hands. Uno popped up out of the grass with something in his mouth.

The boys ran. Uno kept up with them the mile back to the house. John saw them coming and thought Uno looked a little different and was definitely slower than normal. As they approached, he could see that the dog's head was swelling up and that his tongue, hanging limply from the side of his mouth, was three times bigger than it should have been. The dog also carried, John suspected, the corpse of his attacker, or a piece of it at least.

"Mom," yelled John. "Come here."

Marie stepped out onto the porch. "Oh dear," she said.

Fred followed, "What's the matter?"

"Uno met his match," said John.

Clete and Lee began yelling abbreviated versions of the story at about one hundred feet from the house. Uno loped along, holding his head low, dragging the dead snake through the weeds.

Fred reached into his pocket while walking double time across the yard. He immediately grabbed Uno and found the fang holes in the top of his nose. Uno dropped the dead snake from his mouth. The dog fell down and lay still. Fred opened his pocket knife and sliced the dog's nose all the way across the top from lip to lip.

"Clete, Lee," Fred said calmly, "I need water."

Lee stood in shock, frightened by Uno's willingness to be cut. John followed Clete inside for water.

Miles stepped out of the shop to see what the commotion was all about.

Uno's head felt unusually hot, and his eyes were swollen closed to small slits. One of his ears twitched, and his tongue lay lifeless out of his mouth, which seemed as dry as the prairie. The overall shape of Uno's head was growing.

John reached Fred first with a pitcher of water. Marie stood above the patient, holding Lee's shoulders. Lee's tears were flowing freely, and he kept repeating, "If I hadn't called him, Mama."

"Hush now, Lee," Marie said. "You know Uno lives on the edge the way he hunts those snakes. That dog's not happy unless he's dancing with the devil."

"Dump the water right here," Fred said, pointing to a small divot in the yard. By this time, Uno was lying on his side, seemingly unaware of what was happening.

Fred dredged the bottom of the newly made lake and drug out two handfuls of mud. He covered the dog's nose and face with it.

"Keep digging out mud," he said to John.

John joined in covering the dog's face, neck, and ears with mud. When the dog's upper body was completely covered in earth, Fred picked him up.

"John," he said. "Open the cellar door."

John did as he was told. Fred carried the wounded warrior down into the coolness of the small earthen cavern. He laid the dog down in the corner below the shelves of canned vegetables. He stroked Uno's lower half. Uno didn't move.

Fred emerged from the cellar, covered in mud. Lee was crying into his mother's skirt. Clete stood with a bucket of water, not knowing what he should do with it.

"It's in God's hands now," Fred said. "Clete and Lee, I want you to keep that mud fresh and cool on that dog's face and neck till morning. Do you hear?"

"Yes, sir," said Clete.

Lee choked down some snot. "Yes, sir," he said with fear in his voice.

"Will he be alright?" Marie asked.

Fred didn't answer. He shut the cellar door and repeated to Lee, "That mud needs to be wet and cool. Don't let it cake on him, or it ain't helping him anymore. Do you understand?"

"I do," Lee said.

Clete carried the water toward the cellar. Lee followed. The pair descended the steps toward their fallen friend.

Fred walked back into the house. Marie followed.

John saddled up Midge and trotted down the lane toward the rye field. It was business as usual for him.

Miles turned to finish his work on the cattle chute, thinking the dog was done for.

The sun beat down on the world all day long. Clete and Lee held vigil, pulling dirt from the cellar floor, mixing it with water from the bucket, and replacing the mud on Uno when it began to dry. Lee wanted to lay on top of Uno, but Clete wouldn't let him.

"He's half-dead," Clete said. "Let him breathe."

"He's not half-dead," said Lee. "He's not."

Clete said, "I'm gonna go take a whiz. Can you handle it for a while?"

"Yeah," said Lee. "Bring down a candle or something," Lee called as Clete ascended the stairs toward the door. When Clete pushed the cellar door open, sunlight filled the space. Lee gazed down on his friend. He looked terrible. His tongue lay in the dirt . . . motionless and fat. His eyes completely disappeared beneath the mud, and his breathing sounded scratchy and weak. Lee sat up and readjusted his lanky body to lie directly in front of Uno. He held one of Uno's front paws in his hand. "You're gonna be fine, Uno," he said. "That snake didn't get the best of you."

Lunchtime came and Clete returned with a plate of food from Marie and an already burning lantern.

"Here," he said. "Mom wants you to eat." Clete placed the lantern at the foot of the canning shelves. "Be careful with this," he said. "You know how Mom is. Dad insisted you need light to work by, but we don't have any candles.".

"Okay," said Lee. He grabbed the plate and set it down next to him.

"Lee, you should come out for a while," Clete said. "He's got to sleep it off. It's not right to sit in the darkness like this."

"I want to be here when he wakes up," said Lee. "It's my fault he got bit."

Clete bit his lip and ascended the stairs. "I'll check on you later," he said.

"Okay," said Lee. The world beyond the lifted cellar door looked like the opening to heaven. The light blinded Lee, and he shielded his eyes. He lay back down in front of his dog. He put his arm between Uno's front paws and stroked his neck. A small wheeze escaped the dog's throat, and it startled Lee but gave him hope.

"Uno," he said, rising to his knees. The dog didn't move. His breathing was still weak but steady. After a moment of observing, Lee lay down again. "I love you, Uno," he said.

Lee woke to his mother's hand rubbing his shoulder. "Lee," she said. "Wake up, Lee."

His eyes opened to his mother's glow, and he saw she was holding a pillow and blanket.

"Clete's bringing down more water," she said. "Can I sleep here with you?"

"Sure, Mom," he said. "We'd like that."

Marie smiled. "There's only one string attached to this arrangement," she said.

Lee tilted his head the way Uno may have if faced with a puzzle.

"You must eat the food I've brought you to get one of these blankets," she said. "No excuses."

Lee was starving and cold, so the terms seemed agreeable. He scooted away from Uno toward his mom and reached for the plate. She put her arm around him.

"How's our patient?" she asked.

"I can't tell," he said. "He doesn't move. He is still breathing though."

"He's been through a lot, Lee," she said. "You know he's a fighter. Even fighters need their rest."

"I know, Mom," he said. "I'll never forgive myself if he doesn't make it."

Marie pulled him in close. Lee swallowed a bite of his sandwich hard.

"Lee, Uno loves you more than life. Do you know that?"

Lee stared at the dog's ailing body.

"That dog has spent his life protecting you from rattlesnakes," Marie said. "It wasn't a game to him, Lee. He knew those snakes could hurt you, and he wouldn't have that."

"Yeah," he said. "I know."

"There is no greater love than laying down your life for the one you love, Lee," she said. "No greater."

Lee rested his head in the crux of his mother's embrace and closed his eyes to try to stop the tears from falling. He knew his mom was right. Uno loved him and had always protected him. He knew, too, that if he could trade places with Uno right now . . . he would.

Marie blanketed her son in her love, in her arms, and in a quilt. They held each other through the night, each assuming mud duties whenever one of them woke.

Sleep came heavy to the boy; and when he woke, his mother was gone from his side. She had tucked him in under the blankets before leaving. He rubbed his eyes and crawled over toward his patient.

"Uno?" he said to the muddy, furry heap. He saw no response.

He reached for the bucket to make more mud. The cellar door opened, and the room flooded with light. Heavy boots fell on each step; and when Lee's eyes adjusted, he found his father standing with a hand on each knee looking over the dog.

"He's still breathing," Fred said. "That's a good sign, son. A good sign."

"Yeah?" questioned Lee. "You think he'll be okay?"

"Too soon to tell," Fred said. "Maybe by supper. Now, you go upstairs and eat some breakfast. I'll clean Uno up and put some fresh mud on him. He may need another cut on that nose. It's hard to tell with all the mud. Your mama isn't gonna give us a minute's peace until you've had some eggs."

"Are you sure, Dad," he said. "I want to be here when he wakes up."

"If he wakes up . . . it'll be awhile," Fred said. "You did a good job taking care of him, son. Shoo."

Lee reluctantly ascended the stairs. He covered his eyes from the blinding light of morning and made his way to the porch. Mama met him at the door.

"You are a good man, Lee," she said.

Lee didn't know what she was talking about.

"Thanks, Mom," he said. "Thanks for keeping me company last night."

"Sure," she said. "You know Uno is going to be just fine."

"How do you know?" Lee asked.

"Why does God need a rattlesnake-hunting dog in heaven?" she asked. "We got all the snakes down here."

Lee smiled and felt his eyes begin swimming in hope.

— 14 —

If I have faith as a mustard seed,
I will speak to mountains, and they will move;
and nothing will be impossible for me.
Matthew 17:20

Marie placed scrambled eggs before Lee, which he immediately shoveled into his face. The taste of the first bite was wonderful. He didn't notice the flavor of the following bites; he had left his mind down in the cellar with Uno. He finished his plate before Marie was finished serving the meal.

"No, no," she said to Lee. "You sit right there. We are going to talk."

"Yes, ma'am," said Lee, reapplying his hind end to the seat of his chair.

Marie sat next to him and reached for his hands. She held Lee's dirty fingers in hers, "You didn't wash up?"

"I'm sorry, mama," Lee said. "I was hungry."

She shook her head, "Never mind that now. You need to come to terms with two things before Uno wakes up . . . if he wakes up. Are you hearing me?"

Lee asked, "What?"

"One, it is not your fault Uno got bit, whether you called him or not. A boxer doesn't go into the ring listening for his favorite girl to shout. He goes into that ring to fight. If he chooses to fight, he is responsible for focusing on the fight and nothing else. Do you get me?"

"Yes," said Lee.

"Two, if Uno does not wake up, he will be running to the top of heaven's highest hill to be with our God. If we could all be so lucky to find our end at the Lord's feet . . . well, there is no better outcome. And you can count on the fact that when you die a wrinkly old man, that dog is gonna meet you at St. Peter's gate, tail wagging and tongue hanging."

Lee's eyes became leaky, and he forced a smile.

"Yes, Mama," he said.

She summarized, "Repeat after me, 'Not my fault.'"

"Not my fault," Lee said.

"Not the end," she said.

"Not the end," Lee said.

"Now, you go wash those filthy hands and see if your daddy needs help with Uno," she said.

"Thank you, Mama," Lee said. He leaned forward and planted a kiss on top of her head.

"There are no snakes in heaven," she said.

"Not a one," Lee said.

Lee scrubbed up to his elbows and rinsed. He dried his arms on a towel and blew his nose.

He walked out of the house feeling something new—something he couldn't describe. It was as if his mom took his pain and guilt, slathered it with grace, and gave it right back to him as joy and hope. Like the jellied toast he swallowed almost whole, it nourished him.

Lee met his father in the yard. Fred was carrying a very limp, wet dog from the well.

"Follow me," Fred said.

Lee did.

They descended into the earth. Fred lay Uno down near the same spot. The dog was motionless and still breathing heavily. The swelling on his face seemed better, but it was hard to tell what was happening. You still couldn't make out where his eyes were. Lee took a deep breath and said a quick silent prayer for Uno's suffering.

"Look here," Fred said, pointing to Uno's forehead. "I cut him again right there to relieve some of the swelling. It didn't even bleed, which I think is a good thing."

Lee squinted in the low light to see the new cut.

"What I think we should do now is keep on with the mud, but I want you to cover the whole top side of his body down to his ribs. Right here," he said, pointing to Uno's rib cage. "The dog is still feverish, and I think he needs some help fighting it off."

Lee nodded, "I can do that."

"Okay, I also think we should change the mud a little more often . . . maybe every half hour or so," he said.

"I can do that," Lee said.

"I'll ring the supper chime on the porch every thirty minutes," he said. "When you hear it, change the mud. If you don't hear it but think it's time . . . just do it. Okay?"

"Okay," he said.

"I'll check on you in a couple of hours," Fred said.

Lee looked up at his dad, who seemed so in control and so knowledgeable. He wondered if he got his knowledge from experience or from books.

"Thanks, Dad," Lee said.

"You're welcome, son," Fred said. "But it's you who are working to save Uno's life . . . Don't forget to pray, son. In the end, it's in God's hands, and he listens to every word you send him."

Lee smiled.

Thirty minutes didn't seem like enough time to get the mud on, scrape it off, and reapply it. Lee was constantly working. Uno's matted fur was clumping, and Lee suspected it hurt Uno when he pulled the mud off too powerfully. He wanted to be gentle, but with time Lee's anxiety grew about his ability to serve as his friend's caretaker. He kept hoping his dad would come back and help him. He thought about what his mom said. He decided to sing while he worked, "Oh, when the saints . . . are marching in . . . When the saints are marching in . . . Oh, Lord, I want to be in that number . . . when the saints are marching in . . . And when the sun . . . begins to shine . . . And when the sun begins to shine . . . Oh, Lord, I want to be in that number . . . when the saints are marching in . . ."

He realized he didn't know a lot of the words, but he liked the rhythm of what he did know. It occupied his mind and kept him from worrying about his speed.

Hours later, Lee took a break and rubbed his aching fingers. His hands were throbbing, and his shoulders were stiff. He stood and walked around the room. The door opened and light flooded the scene. Lee squinted, adding eye pain to his list of complaints.

"Dad?" he said.

"No, dummy," said John. "It's me."

"Oh," said Lee. "What are you doing here?"

"What do you think?" he said. "I'm checking on Uno."

John kneeled next to the dog and felt the dog's face and head. "Well, his tongue is certainly smaller," said John. "It's been about twenty hours," he said. "We should know soon."

"That's what Dad said too," Lee said.

John looked at him sideways. "You take a break," he said. "You look awful. Go take a nap or something."

"I want to be here when he wakes up," said Lee.

"I promise you it will be a while," said John. "Go."

Lee climbed the stairs back to the world and realized he had been down there all day. He could hear the cicadas warming up and knew John was right. He was tired. Lee approached his dad sitting in the porch chair.

"How is he?" Fred asked.

"Same," Lee said. "I think the same. John thinks his tongue is smaller than yesterday."

"Well," Fred said, "that's a good sign. Check in with your mother."

"Okay," said Lee.

Marie met Lee at the screen door.

"Clean up first this time," she said.

"Yes, ma'am," Lee said.

Lee scrubbed to his elbows. His mother brought him some clean clothes, and he left his muddy nurse's uniform on the washroom floor. Freshly clothed and somewhat clean, he sat at the table and ate the food he was given. He could barely keep his eyes open.

His mother finally said, "Lee, go to bed."

He walked toward the stairway but later wouldn't remember crawling into bed.

He found his slice of mattress and noticed some of Uno's fur stuck to the covers. He laid his face down on Uno's spot and could smell the dog lingering in the blanket. He slept hard. He didn't know how long. It was nighttime when he woke and realized Clete was lying on top of his legs.

"Clete," he said, "move. I gotta go."

The weight didn't lift from his legs.

"Clete," he yelled, "wake up. I gotta check on Uno."

Suddenly the weight rose from his legs, and he felt it step on his thigh. Lee, finally waking, reached out to Clete. "What are you doing? Get off me."

Lee's fingers reached to push Clete off but instead felt a thin furry leg. It was too thin and too furry to belong to Clete. It was Uno.

"Uno!" Lee yelled. Uno licked Lee's face over and over. The dog barked a single bark. Lee reached out to hug his dog and felt Uno's head. The swelling was almost completely gone, and someone who didn't know the story may think he tangled with a bobcat. The two cuts on his face looked traumatic, but Uno didn't seem to notice them.

Fred walked in the room. "So are you getting reacquainted?"

"Oh, Fred, thank you so much," Lee said.

"You did it, Lee," Fred said. "He was pretty much better a couple of hours into your nap. We didn't want to wake you, so we let him come up here to you, so he could be here when YOU woke up."

Lee hugged the dog and lay back down in his bed. Uno waited for Lee to get comfortable and then found a spot for himself next to him. Uno laid his head down on Lee's chest. Licking his own nose for a couple of minutes, Uno yawned and then settled down on top of his friend.

Lee was too excited to sleep. Uno fell into sleep almost immediately.

Everyone in the family came to check on them at some point of the night and early morning. Lee smiled in his sleep and woke to Uno's sloppy kisses. The pair shared a hearty breakfast of bacon and eggs.

After breakfast, Uno jumped right back in the saddle by cornering a rattlesnake near the barn. Lee grabbed him as soon as he saw him assume the battle position.

"Not today you don't," said Lee, dragging him back into the house.

"Mom," he said. "Uno wants to go after snakes already."

Marie smiled, "Fighters fight, Lee."

"Well, I'm not ready to let him fight. We're going upstairs for a while."

"Okay," said Marie. "I don't blame you."

Marie spent the day doing housework and cleaning. She was pleased Uno pulled through. It would have been devastating to Lee had it gone the other way. She laughed every time she heard Uno's tail wag against the floorboards. Thunk, thunk, thunk, thunk . . . and Lee's laughter singing harmony. It was music to her ears.

15

. . . Behold, Satan hath desired to have you, that he may sift you as wheat:
But I have prayed for thee, that thy faith fail not.
Luke 22:31–32 (King James Version)

As grain and livestock prices fell by half and unemployment was wide-spread in the cities, Nebraska succumbed to the Great Depression. Because things had been unofficially tough in McCloud Valley for some time, national affairs didn't seem to spark much dinner conversation. The McClouds had hope they would get credit for time served. It seemed John's and Miles' work was beginning to pay off, and in 1932–33 the crops were favorable. If you didn't consider the profit as payment by the hours of labor, it was tolerable. In 1934 there was a great rye crop in the field just west of the house. However, it was the last profitable crop the McClouds ever planted. It was that same year when the winds blew stronger and the earth shriveled up and died beneath everyone's feet. The clouds refused to rain, and the sun baked everything, living and dead, until it broke into tiny pieces and blew away.

One Sunday just after arriving home from mass, John was standing in the yard. Fred was on the porch enjoying a day of rest. It was a clear, hot day with no wind. Toward the lower end of McCloud Valley, John noticed a reddish cloud low on the horizon. Its leading edge was flat as a board. As it approached and rose over the valley, you could see from top to bottom it was a dark-bronze rolling, boiling mass of dirt.

"Everybody inside," John yelled. This dust cloud was ten times the size of anything the valley had ever seen.

Uno barked and herded the kids toward the house. Fred was the last to enter. He shut the screen door, and the girls began shoving wet towels, pillow cases, and blankets into every window, door frame, and possible entry point. Hearts pounded, and Marie's rosary beads began to click. A chicken's cry broke the tension. Everyone followed the sound to Uno's mouth. He brought dinner.

Light disappeared from the world as the storm approached, as if the sun plummeted from the sky. Small ticks of sound began clicking on the house until it grew into a constant roar. Early on, Fred lost sight of the barn across the yard. Eventually the posts on the porch railing were hidden from view, and Fred's chair crashed across the porch and relocated to Ray Johnson's porch three miles away.

The storm lasted hours. The family tried to enjoy their fried chicken, courtesy of Uno. The time was spent in as normal a way as possible; Bible reading and bedtimes were maintained. No one seemed to sleep, however, until the onslaught relented.

The valley woke to land covered in red dust, like sifted flour. It drifted like snow in the typical locations but was three feet deep across the yard. Fence lines were drifted over, and the cattle that still lived, moved freely to answer for themselves if the proverbial grass was greener on the other side. People said the red soil came from Oklahoma, which made perfect sense by the texture and color. The riddle of it was that it flew in from the north.

It put an end to any and all crops, which were covered too heavily to get sunlight—not that they were getting any water. John felt something inside him break. He kept it to himself and had a hard time coming to terms with what the world was doing. In a moment, for the first time, he saw a little of Fred in himself. He felt pure hopelessness.

John, Clete, Lee, and Fred worked outside to clean the place up. Given the soft texture of the soil, it was a difficult task. It got into every nook and cranny of all the equipment and dusted everything in the barn. Big, who was normally black, and Shorty, who was normally white, were now gingerbread twins. Their nostrils were caked with soil, and they coughed and wheezed for a week. The cow wore a similar shade. The first time John milked her, he couldn't decide if the milk was tinged with red, cinnamon-flavored, or if he hadn't gotten the bucket clean enough.

Marie insisted on coating everyone's nostrils in Vaseline and then covering everything but the eyes with a wet dish towel. She felt the dust would stick to the Vaseline and not enter the body as a person breathed. Burying one child was where she drew the line. John was convinced the Vaseline was a magnet and rather than breathe in dust particles you got to choke down boulders of gooey, sticky Oklahoma mud. Whether it proves anything or not, Marie never nursed a child through dust pneumonia.

The girls worked with their mother to sweep and wash and clean the house. No matter how many clothes and blankets they stuffed in the cracks, the dirt got in. It clung to fabric curtains, bed linens, light fixtures, and dishes. Uno shook himself clean several times and always seemed to get rid of the same amount of dust.

Fred set up a ladder to sweep out the gutters of the house and realized it was a silly, if valiant, cause. The rain hadn't come in so long he thought the gutters could be retired without too much notice. He did the job without complaint. From the roof of the house, he got a good look at the valley. He had never seen the likes of this storm. He felt as if his heart broke, not sure if the end of the world was coming . . . or if it was just the end of him. He coughed up phlegm and blood and a mud pie all in one fit. No one noticed, so he went on with the business of cleaning.

It took two weeks of dedicated effort to get the place recognizable. The only new feature on the homestead was a mound of Oklahoma tucked in behind the barn: a souvenir from a trip never taken.

John began sleeping harder through the night and having a harder time getting up in the morning. He didn't know if it was his imagination or not, but everyone in the family seemed to be getting thinner. Even Uno seemed a bit on the tender side. He tried to work through each day as if nothing was different but knew it was a farce. Everyone was wearing the same mask of normality.

It was a time of disappointment when the phantom rainstorms came. The clouds formed thunderheads and roared belligerent rumbles throughout the valley. A smell of rain floated through the air, and lightning shattered the sky. With the storm overhead and the expectation of an end to the foreplay, every farmer in the Midwest danced and threw their hats in the air. Soon enough the smell of rain would be replaced by the smell of brimstone and sulfur created by the lightning. The air was charged with electricity, and shaking a man's hand could leave you on your ass.

The lightning storms were hard on the livestock too. The instinct of most farm animals is to escape flies by heading to the hilltops; the wind would blow stronger there, keeping the flies at bay. Of course, they escaped the flies and gambled with the lightning, which always struck high spots. Sometimes the bolt left entry and exit burns on the animal; most times it didn't. Fred used to say that if the beast had horns, the horns would be shook loose. John was never able to confirm or deny that fact; and since the family didn't own any animals with horns, it was useless information.

Prayer was a big thing in the McCloud home in good times. In the bad times, prayer was relentless. Marie would gather the children in the family room during storms and pray, "Deliver us from this thunder and lightning, Lord. Deliver us from this storm," over and over and over again. At any given moment, someone in the home was praying, preparing to pray, or thinking about praying. Marie led the family, and John only prayed when Marie cornered him to do so.

They were tough years for everyone but hardest, Fred felt, on the Catholics. Church was never missed. The family could choose mass in Merna or Anselmo. For the variety, it seemed to alternate week to week. Father Kellen, in Anselmo, was a good man but one of the old school. He had a booming voice and loved to hear it. Mass, benediction, and a long sermon could take anywhere from an hour and a half to two hours. Fred used to say a Catholic can get his money's worth with Father Kellen.

Despite a shortage of gas on the farm, there was always something in the tank to get to church. Father Kellen enjoyed hosting mission priests, which included evening services three nights in a row. With four services under the belt at week's end, it is a wonder the farm didn't just float right up to heaven. Everyone seemed to enjoy church, but in their own way and for their own reasons.

Marie was a true believer, an Irish Catholic woman of faith. Fred enjoyed the socializing. John enjoyed getting off the farm and checking out the skirts. Angela, Elaine, and Lucy were coming of age to be courted; so in addition to their salvation, perusing the landscape of suitors was a bonus activity. Clete and Lee just loved being part of the family. Clete was a talker and had a hard time sitting still throughout the services. Lee was a people watcher and enjoyed the music. He could hum a tune with the same fervor a priest could describe your personal route to hell. Uno didn't go to church, which always seemed disappointing to Lee and Uno both. Lee would watch him follow the Model T down the lane, and Uno would stop at the corner and sit, watching until they were out of sight.

Lee had always assumed Uno continued living his life between their departure and their arrival home. But on the rare occasions John didn't go to mass, he reported Uno to be standing guard at the lane's end throughout the extent of the family's absence.

It was a typical Sunday drive home from church, when a black cloud formed on the horizon behind them. Fred floored the Model T, which brought it up to about a jog. The kids stared out the back of the vehicle keeping tabs on the cloud, which was clearly and easily gaining on them. Everyone but John was in the vehicle. They reached the end of their lane when the cloud fell on them. They decided to get out and run. Hand-in-hand, the McClouds—plus Uno, minus John— forged their way up the lane. The cloud seemed different. It sounded different. It buzzed. Uno leapt up and nipped at things, crunching as if he'd earned a treat.

John was on horseback in the south pasture. He saw the dark curtain falling across the land and headed for home. Midge galloped through the field, and John noticed that the cloud rose straight up in the air like a tidal wave. It had speed and mass, and Midge seemed spooked. He kept her focused with a click of his heels in her side. They reached the barn just after the family realized it wasn't a dust cloud. It was grasshoppers. They fell hard like hail and either clung to your hair or used you as leverage to leap away. Both feelings left you a little uneasy, especially at the rate it was happening.

Fred yelled, "In the barn."

Everyone flew in behind Midge, who was crawling out of her skin. Her tail was swishing, and she was turning back on her reins to shake herself free of the insects. Fred and Angela drug the barn doors shut, and Clete ran up to the top floor to close the hay door.

"What the hell is it?" said Fred.

"Damn grasshoppers," said John.

"It's a plague," said Marie.

"It's not a damn plague, Ma," said John.

"You watch that language, John Francis McCloud," Marie said.

"Sorry, Ma," John said.

The girls groomed each other like monkeys, picking the crawling, tangled things out of their hair, their church dresses. Lee brushed his hand along Uno, who didn't seem to mind the company he had hitching a ride on him. Uno licked at them on Lee's clothes and gobbled them up as soon as he could manage to chew them.

It was an hour before the buzzing quieted. Fred and John climbed up to the hay door and opened it for a peek. The land was covered in leaping, chewing khaki and black grasshoppers. A few still flew through the air, although they could see the cloud had continued past them toward the south.

The men sat on either side of the hay door, speechless.

"What do you see?" shouted Elaine.

"Grasshoppers," said Fred. "And lots of 'em."

"The cloud is past us," said John. "Looks like we got the dropouts."

"Well, we can't live in the barn," said Marie.

Lee disagreed. He enjoyed the barn. He and Uno wrestled in a pile of hay.

John sat at the hay door stunned.

Fred returned to the main level of the barn.

"It's gonna get dark in here pretty soon," he said. "Your mama is right. Let's go."

Everyone looked at each other. No one moved.

John descended from above, "Come on now. They are grasshoppers. They aren't gonna eat you."

He strode past with the confidence of a man about to pick up his first paycheck.

As the barn door groaned open, a window into the new normal took shape. John turned to face the kids, and seeing their faces process what was out there was heart wrenching. He could see the girls were fearful and on the verge of tears. Clete and Lee seemed stunned yet able to accept this never-seen-before event. John watched them adjust to the idea of living in a creeping, crawling world. The girls reached for each other's hands. Clete grabbed Lee's hand. Uno ambled past John out into the yard. He stopped midway to the house and turned to look back at the barn as if to say, "What are you waiting for?"

Marie put herself between Clete and Lee and took the first step outside. Lucy, Elaine, and Angela followed. John followed. Fred watched his brood hustle into the house, and he moved over to shut the barn door . . . except he stayed inside. The door was open long enough that he was joined by a committee of hopping, flying, chewing, and buzzing company.

He found a spot on a pile of straw, sat down in it, and stared up at the ceiling.

"God help us," he said as a twitch erupted near his eye.

16

Moreover if your brother sins against you,
go and tell him his fault between you and him alone.
If he hears you, you have gained your brother.
But if he will not hear, take with you one or two more,
that 'by the mouth of two or three witnesses every word may be established.
Matthew 18:15–16 (King James Version)

The remainder of the day was very solemn, moods were quiet, and the house was very hot. Temperatures had been holding steadily in the hundreds; and with no air conditioning or electricity for a fan, everyone was covered in a sheen of moisture. Mother Nature was stripping away any and all comforts of life. Marie approached windows several times to let some air in but each time found layers of grasshoppers coating the outside frame. It didn't take long for her to notice the paint disappearing.

John approached Marie in the kitchen.

"Fred is still in the barn," said John. "Do we leave him there?"

"I don't know," said Marie. "This is a blow to all of us, but your father is fragile."

"Hmm," said John. "He's lazy, Ma, not fragile."

"Respect your father, John Francis," she said sternly.

"Well, should I check on him?" he said. "I can't skip milking tonight, and I'm about to go. The old girl is probably already painful 'cause I skipped this morning for the well work," John said. "I figured you were fretting about him and thought I could check on him for you if you like. How about I send you a signal to ease your heart, Ma?"

"What do you mean?" Marie asked.

"If Fred is fine I'll lean a pitchfork against the barn door," said John. "If he's not, I'll be in like a racehorse."

"John," Marie said. "What would I do without you?"

"I don't know," said John. "But soon enough you're gonna find out. I'll be old enough to leave in a couple of years, and I'm planning on it. You need to start thinking. If Clete and Lee can't step up to take over, you'll need to move to town."

Marie knew it was true.

"I'll talk to Clete shortly," she said. "But who wants to farm in a world like this . . . maybe we can take the grasshoppers to market."

John smiled, "Now you're thinking."

John's boots fell heavily down the hall toward the door. Marie drifted behind him. She watched John cross the yard, swatting at grasshoppers as he went. He entered the barn, swinging the door wide. She inhaled, wringing a dish towel in her hands. Grasshoppers began gripping the screen door and blocking her view. She adjusted her gaze each time her vision seemed sketchy. John hadn't returned with a pitch fork, and the dish towel cut off the circulation to her fingers. She could feel the tingle of starvation in it but couldn't move. John was taking too long. Even if Fred had been sleeping, he could have been roused and moving by now. Panic moved through her mind.

A pair of boots exited the barn . . . but not the boots she was expecting. It was John carrying Fred in his arms. Fred's mouth hung open, and blood stained his teeth and face.

Marie pushed the screen door open and ran out to meet John. "Is he breathing?" she asked.

"I think so," John sputtered. "Get the door."

Marie rushed ahead and swung the screen. John angled sideways down the hall toward his parents' bedroom. He plopped Fred down on the bed and backed away so his mama could do her inspection.

"Call Doc Stone," she said.

"Let's figure out what's wrong first," John said.

"Now," she said.

John exited the room to call the doctor.

Marie called for Angela to bring in wet washcloths. She worked to swat off the grasshoppers that clung to his clothes and hair.

"What happened?" Angela asked.

"I don't know," Marie said. "John found him in the barn."

The blood was centered on his nose. As Marie cleaned the blood away, she couldn't find a logical explanation. He was there alone, so a brawl was out. If it were just a bloody nose, he wouldn't be unconscious. She racked her brain for explanations . . . finding none, she was short on solutions.

He didn't seem feverish or painful, but she couldn't get him to wake up. "Fred," she said, slapping his cheeks. "Come on, Fred."

"John," Marie said. "Come here."

John came and stood in the doorway. "Stone is on his way."

"Tell me how you found him," she said.

"He was lying in a pile of hay," John said.

"Face down or up?" she asked.

"Down," John said. "Maybe he fell."

"Or had a seizure," Marie said, deciding to work around that hypothesis until something more likely came up.

"May I be excused?" John asked. "I can milk until Stone arrives. I'll walk him in."

"Fine," Marie said. "Thank you, John."

John left.

Elaine and Lucy stood in the doorway, anxious over what was happening.

Clete and Lee were upstairs and yet unaware of any activity.

"Should I get the boys?" Elaine asked.

"No," said Marie. "No need to worry them yet."

John stomped to the barn, crushing grasshoppers in his path. He left the barn door open for light. He approached the cow with his bench and buckets and quickly got to work.

Fred came alive with a jump. He pushed Marie away from him. "Where's John?" he asked.

"Milking," Marie said. "He found you in the barn."

"Seizures or not, I'm the man of this house. He and I need to talk," said Fred.

Fred walked toward the barn with determined steps. He picked up a board that was leaning against the door frame of the barn. John was still milking the cow with his head facing away from the barn door. His face was leaning into the cow's side as his arms stretched to get at the teats farthest from him.

John was pumping the milk into a bucket with a consistent rhythm when he lost a grip on one of the teats. In the silence of that interruption, he heard a boot step behind him. He turned his head and saw a board coming down on him. John immediately launched from the bench. The board fell hard on the wooden stool, and John grabbed the wood board and shoved it as hard as he could back into the stomach of his attacker. He forced the board back, stepping forward several times. He heard the man lose his breath. He pushed him into the wall of the barn, leaning into the board with all his weight. Finally, he looked up to see the contorted, red face of his father. With renewed strength, he forced the board into his stomach and tried to twist it without losing his grip.

"John," Fred gasped.

John let go of the board, and it fell to the ground. Dust particles flew up into the air and danced around the pair like gnats on a horse's ass. Fred coughed, wheezed, and gasped, holding his stomach and hunching over. Grasshoppers leapt onto him, over him, and off of him.

John stared at his father, waiting for him to recover. His eyes sliced him into pieces as Fred spit on the barn floor.

After a deep inhale, Fred put a hand on each knee and lifted himself to John's glare.

"If you ever try that again," said John, "I will kill you."

John let silence punctuate his message.

Fred stood straight, flinching with the effort.

"This isn't your farm," said Fred. "I am the man of this family. You need to stop acting like you run the place."

John laughed aloud. "I do run the place. If you want the job, stand up and do it."

Fred stepped toward John. "I can't change my health, John. I do what I can. I think you need to get about leaving," Fred said.

Marie stood in the doorway. She stepped in and stood between the men.

"First off," she said, eyeing them both equally. "If I EVER find you boys throwing fists or fighting again, it's lye soap for both of you . . . for a month."

John continued murdering Fred in his mind.

Fred imagined John walking down the lane.

"Secondly," she said, addressing Fred. "Your seizures forced you to give up the responsibility of running this farm years ago. John is in charge of this farm as of now. If you can step up, stay healthy, and prove yourself, you may resume control of operations when John leaves, AT HIS DESIRE TO DO SO."

"Am I clear?" she said.

Fred said nothing.

Turning to John, she said. "Finally, I will not tolerate you being disrespectful to your father. If I catch or hear a hint of arrogance or belittling or poking fun at your father again, you will be leaving at MY desire. I mean it, John—not a single solitary word or look against your father. His seizures are life threatening and certainly not his choice. If the doctors ever find a treatment for it, Fred will be first in line to get it. Until then, not a single word about it, John."

"Am I clear?" she said.

John looked at her as if she had switched heads with a goat.

"We will not have this conversation again," she said. "None of this will be spoken of to anyone living on or off this farm. If one of the other children gets wind of it and our arrangement, you will both be gone."

Marie stood between the men, head held high, cheeks boiling with rage, voice controlled with righteousness.

"As God is my witness," she said. "You will both do as I command, or you will face my wrath."

Neither man spoke, but their faces began to relax. Clenched fists fell apart finger by finger.

"Now, you will both enter that home and socialize with your emotionally tattered family for the remainder of the day. You will smile. You will laugh. And you will spend every waking minute worrying about soothing their minds. Do you hear me?" she said.

Neither man spoke.

"I will have angels flying out my ass before the two of you will sully my mood again," she said.

She raged internally like a bonfire crackling. Neither of the men had seen her this way before. The three of them stood looking at each other for a few moments, as the men focused on swallowing their resentment, pride, and anger.

"Shall we?" she said, ushering the men toward the full buckets of milk still under and near the cow. They each picked one up and turned toward the barn door.

"Stop right there," Marie said. They did.

"Put those buckets down," she said. They did.

"Let's practice a happy mug," she said. "If I don't get satisfaction, we will stay in this barn hugging and singing Kumbayah until I get it."

Their teeth broke out like headlights on a car.

"Cover those buckets with your hats," she said. They did.

"You first," she said to the toothy duo.

They moved forward as if in a marching band. Marie followed closely, smiling at the feel of her Irish leaping through her veins.

John held the door open for Fred. Fred said, "Thank you."

John said, "You're welcome."

Marie walked through the screen door with a laughter building up in her that could blow at any second. She sauntered down the hall and entered her bedroom, closing the door behind her. She reached for a pillow and laughed into it. The sound was muffled, but even if the whole world heard her, it was worth it.

She collected herself, smoothed her hair and apron, and opened the bedroom door. Uno was the only one who seemed to share any knowledge of her outburst, and she swore he gave her a nod as if to say, "Well done, Ma."

"I want everyone picking up grasshoppers and putting them in this flour sack," she said. Marie picked up the phone to call the doctor back and cancel his trip.

John and Fred leapt to attention and began scouring the rooms for insects. Fred held the sack; John hunted the grasshoppers. The other children slowly picked themselves up and were stunned at the sudden teamwork between John and Dad. No one commented on it. The grasshoppers were collected, all but one. Lee adopted one whom he found to be incredibly special. He kept him in a shoebox, which he held in his arms as the hunters gathered their prey.

"What should I name my grasshopper?" Lee asked as John and Fred came by.

"What about Hoppy," Fred said. Lee scrunched up his face and shook his head no.

"What about Balls?" suggested John. Lee tilted his head.

"Why Balls?" Lee asked.

"Well, it's a lucky day," said John. "You found a grasshopper, and Ma found a couple of balls out in the barn."

Fred blew snot out of his nose.

"What kind of balls?" Lee asked. "Can I play with them?"

"Oh no," said Fred. "They're not the kind of balls you want anything to do with."

"I like Balls," said Lee. And so Balls the grasshopper lived a very comfortable life on the top floor of the McCloud home for the next two weeks. Balls came to a quiet and mysterious end, as he escaped his shoebox without leaving a clue to his method of departure or his reasons for leaving.

Fred said he probably went to California to find work, like all the other "Okies".

It seemed as good an end as any, so Lee moved on to find another "special" grasshopper.

— 17 —

Have mercy on me, O Lord, for I am weak;
O Lord, heal me, for my bones are troubled.
Psalm 6:2

It seemed as though Uno and Angela were the only "officially" work-ing members of the family; Angela was teaching at District 222 School, which was known as McCloud School as a result of Grandpa Robert McCloud's donation of the land. Unfortunately, the school district went broke, so Angela was collecting IOUs for her time. Uno got a hankering for jackrabbits. Everyone was relieved because they were safer prey than rattle snakes, which became more of a side dish than a main course.

Occasionally Marie sent Clete and Lee out to follow Uno on the hunt so they could collect some of his trophies for dinner. Rabbit stew was long on rabbit, long on broth, shorter on everything else. The supply of canned vegetables in the cellar was depleted. The garden was buried beneath two and a half feet of dust, and the big wildlife was being hunted by every hungry man in the area. It had been close to a year since a wild turkey or deer had been seen on the property. The coyotes had been enjoyed with a side of bread, which was baked with the last of 1934's crop. In the absence of the coyote, jackrabbits had become kings, feasting on the plentiful supply of grasshoppers, fence posts, tar paper, and wood. After the first grasshopper tour, it looked as if everyone in the valley had put in new cedar fence posts; they were eaten clean to a smooth finish.

Some families were getting together for picnics called rabbit drives to corner and club as many jacks as possible. It seemed to be a crime against nature, not to mention Easter. The McClouds would have none of it. Uno was the best rabbit deterrent God could have designed. The dog was fatter than he'd ever been, despite putting in long hours of sniper duty and many miles underfoot. Everyone noticed Uno filling out, and it just didn't add up—jackrabbits or not.

In contrast, his favorite human, Lee, was withering. The child who had always held a lanky, slender frame was becoming skeletal. Lee had no energy. Dark swags of skin hung below a pair of hollow, sunken eyes. His demeanor remained pleasant and cheerful, but the child was clearly suffering.

Uno, who seemed to sense a change in Lee, slowed his pace to match Lee's ability and speed. Finally, Clete began pulling his little brother around the farm with a Radio Flyer coaster wagon. Marie was beside herself with worry. Polio had been rearing its ugly head, and her nightmares were filled with it. She called Doc Stone, who came out to examine Lee. Doc looked in Lee's mouth, nose, and ears. He felt Lee's throat, chest, stomach, and legs. Then Doc sat quietly for some time rubbing his chin with the fingers of one hand. Finally, slapping his hands down on his thighs, he decided it wasn't polio that gripped Lee.

Marie was shocked, having already convinced herself it was polio. She stood slack jawed with eyebrows raised.

"He's not eating," said Doc.

Offended, Marie insisted he was, "I feed that child more than the others, hoping he'll snap out of it."

"Well, then, I suspect you have a big, fat dog," Doc said, closing his medical bag, snapping the clutch, and standing up.

"Lee," he said, "are you going to tell us what's going on with your food?"

Lee looked from an already furious mom to the local physician and back to mom. The jig was up. Uno waddled out of the room, abandoning the loving, quick hand that had fed him vegetables consistently for months. Lee watched him go through the door and turn to look at

110

him. Pausing for only a moment, the dog continued down the stairs and to his favorite spot, behind the wood-burning stove.

"I hate vegetables," Lee said.

"You'll be hating them a lot more when I'm through with you," said Marie.

"Looks like it's spinach and carrots for you, my son," Doc said. "Now understand, Lee, this is not to be taken lightly. You eat."

"Yes, sir," said Lee.

Marie left the room with a cloud of rage hanging in the air.

Lee sat on his bed wondering what fate might befall him. He listened to Doc examine Mom's hands, which had been giving her fits lately. He told her to find some liniment oil or aloe to rub into them. He said, keep 'em clean so they don't infect. He offered to wrap them in gauze to help shield them from the world. Of course, Marie declined.

"Bandages will only get in my way," she said. "I have work to do."

"If you start feeling a fever, you call me," he said.

Lee heard their footsteps descend the stairs; and by the time Doc closed his vehicle door, feet were falling hard on the steps and coming his way. Boots thundered toward Lee, and he shuddered in preparation of the pending lecture. He hated eating green things and already felt ill imagining it. Marie returned with John and Elaine.

"Lee," she said, "John and Elaine are going to figure out where we can plant a garden that will grow. YOU will eat what I feed you. YOU will finish every last bite. YOU will lick the plate if I desire it."

"Do you understand me?" she said.

"Yes, ma'am," Lee said.

"If I catch you feeding that dog again," she said. "Uno will be gone . . . sent to Uncle Bill's place. Is that clear?"

Lee sat horrified.

"Yes, ma'am," he stammered.

"Okay, John, Elaine, come with me," she said.

Everyone left the room, and only John gave Lee a backward glance. It seemed uncertain if John would yell too or just laugh. John was sometimes hard to read. Lee lay back on the bed. He couldn't imagine Uno having to live with Uncle Bill. He knew Uno didn't like him and the way he spat tobacco like a shotgun. Far be it for the man to find a can or something to spit in; the world was his spittoon. Each time they had visited Uncle Bill, Uno came home with lumps of stinky brown spittle in his fur. The dog spent hours twisting his head back over himself trying to reach the shrapnel that poisoned his smooth black coat.

Lee lay down on the bed letting his mind quietly search for sleep.

Marie, John, and Elaine walked across the yard straight to the barn.

"We need a greenhouse, Ma," said John.

"We don't have any wood," she said.

"We're surrounded by wood," he said. "Look at the barn; we could take out a stall, a wall, something . . ."

"No, we need to keep that barn intact for the good times," she said. "There will be good times, John. God has promised."

John bit his lip hard enough for it to turn purple.

Elaine said, "What about the casing on the well? It's just for show anyway, isn't it?"

Marie paused. Everyone halted. Mom kick-started into the barn, John and Elaine tailing her.

Lee woke to a scratching noise. He rolled over to find his fair-weather friend Uno scratching on the door. The dog had a jack in his mouth. He dropped it and picked it up again only to drop it more powerfully.

"Eat, Lee, eat," Lee imagined him saying.

"I need veggies," spat Lee. "Mom will skin you if she finds a dead rabbit in her house. You better get."

The dog picked up the jack and disappeared down the stairs. Lee heard Uno push the screen door open with his nose and pad off in search of veggies (or so he imagined).

Lee was having a hard time keeping his eyes open. He was so tired. So weak. He really didn't feel sick—just exhausted and a little cramped up. Maybe he needed his own bed. It would do wonders to not wake up with John's elbow in an ear and one of Clete's heels in his backside. Lee's eyelids bounced until his lashes stuck closed.

John, Elaine, Lucy, Angela, and Clete gathered in the barn with

Marie and Fred.

Fred said, "Let's scour this place to find some materials for a greenhouse."

"What about that old windmill up the road," John said. "It doesn't work anymore . . . well is dry."

"John, it's not our windmill," said Fred.

"They aren't using it," John said.

Fred shook his head and said nothing.

"What about the windows from that abandoned house near the school," Angela said.

"Great idea," Marie said.

"Well, that house isn't ours either," said John.

"Noted," said Fred. "But we know they are long gone to Texas and most likely aren't coming back."

John shifted his weight from one foot to the other, hands on his hips. "How are we gonna keep the grasshoppers, dirt, and rocks from blowing right through a window?"

"We'll cover it somehow when storms come," said Marie.

"We could take out the pocket doors of the house if we can live without some privacy," said John.

"Great idea," said Clete.

"What about the cattle chute," said Lucy.

"Done," said Marie.

"We'll need some wire and nails," said Fred.

"I can get those," said John.

Everyone turned up an eyebrow, but no one spoke.

"Let's break up into teams," said Marie.

"Fred, work with Clete; John, with Lucy; Elaine, with Angela; Uno and I will scour the house," Marie said. "Collect everything you think we might need as you come across it. Bring it to the south side of the house."

As the teams broke off in different directions, John and Lucy headed to the barn, whispering all the way. Big and Shorty appeared with the scavengers riding bareback. John had an ax hidden in his lap, and

Lucy had a hammer.

Fred and Clete went to dismantle the cattle chute. For some reason, they couldn't find the hammer, so they tried to make do with a chisel. Elaine and Angela went toward the family's own windmill. Marie went back into the house and peeked in at Lee to find him sleeping so deeply the grim reaper would have had to wait for Lee to come around before taking him. The reaper, it seemed, would also have had to get past Uno, who lay guarding his sickly master. The dog covered Lee's chest with his snout and let his tail wag twice as Marie entered.

She nodded her acknowledgement to Uno and knelt down in the doorway of the bedroom. She didn't reach for her rosary. She was gonna have a personal, wet-eyed, heart-wrenching talk with her Lord. She placed her hands together and began . . .

"Heavenly Father, I know you are putting out a lot of fires right now, and I don't mean to be a burden. I promise you that I'm not gonna ask you for rain. I'm not asking for a cool breeze. I'm not praying for the grasshoppers and jacks to move along. I don't care if the stock market ever recovers, the crops ever grow . . . You can send all the dust your will requires. I surrender my life and my children's lives to you."

Marie paused, collecting her thoughts and wiping her eyes of moisture. She squeezed her cracked, weary hands together, and a drop of blood fell onto the floor.

"Please, Lord, don't take my baby home. Lee is my little boy, and he ain't done growin' yet. God, please allow him time. I can see he's fading. I know in my mother's gut that he ain't gonna last long enough for a seed to grow into anything worth eating. Please, God, I only ask for some fruit or some vegetables. I know your business is your own, and I understand your will is the way. But I wouldn't be doing your work if I just lay down and watched him blow away with the dust. You gave him to me. I'm not ready to give him to you. Please, Heavenly Father, send me one orange or one carrot. I'm asking for one fruit or vegetable and the time for Lee to eat it. You have my Joey. Lord, I don't think I can handle losing another child. If you must add a McCloud to your list, add me."

She sat down on her calves and wept. Uno raised his head looking her way. Marie noticed blood drops shining on the hardwood floor. She wiped them up with her apron, pulled herself up, and went looking for materials for the greenhouse.

Lee listened to her haggard soul unravel down the stairs. He could tell from the sound of her movements that she was supporting herself on the wall with each step. He knew from her prayer that he was in deeper than he realized. His fingers moved to his rib cage, and he felt the space between each bone. Fear filled him, and yet he couldn't keep sleep from taking him.

18

Love your neighbor as yourself.
There is no commandment greater...
Mark 12:31

John and Lucy approached the neighbor's windmill. It was very old and dry, a lot like its owner. It stood rotting year after year. John slid off Big with the ax in hand. He started chopping on one angled leg of the structure. It didn't take long for the whole thing to come crashing down. Clouds of dust flew into the air, and the pair coughed and sputtered through it as it settled.

Lucy and John worked to break apart pieces of the "less-rotted" wood. It didn't take long for each of them to have a couple of pockets full of worn, crooked nails and a stack of tolerable boards.

"I'll come back with the wagon," said John.

"I can't believe we did this," said Lucy.

"Ah, the old Dutchman won't miss it," John said. "Besides, we did it for Lee."

"Amen to that," said Lucy.

The two leapt up on their horses forgetting about the nails in their pockets. Big and Shorty both got a scrape, and John and Lucy had a couple of new drainage holes. After much deliberation, John took his hat off, and the nails were transported safely there rather than risk more bodily injury.

By the time they got back, the pile had grown into a respectable mound of materials: two pocket doors; Fred's broken porch chair, which he had retrieved from Ray Johnson's place; some freshly cleaned cedar fence posts; and a recently retired Radio Flyer wagon.

John gave his hat to Lucy to add to the stock while he hitched up the team to the wagon. Without mentioning it, he slipped Lucy's hammer over the tailgate and dropped the ax in with it. He rode off into the afternoon sun. John decided to ride the fence lines nearby. He was out in the south pasture when he rode upon Fred Bates's property border. It was fenced, as John would have expected; but what surprised John was that Fred was storing a few rolls of wire and some posts near the fence. He borrowed a roll of it.

John headed home with his acquisition tucked into the back of his wagon when he came upon Fred Bates's son Ralph. Ralph rode over as though he wanted to talk to John, and the guilt started rolling up to John's temples.

"Good afternoon," Ralph said.

"Hi there," John replied.

"We've lost a couple of cows," Ralph said. "Have you seen 'em?"

"Na, but I ain't been looking I guess," John said. "Are they marked?"

"Yeah," he said. "God knows why we made 'em suffer. They're just skin and bones anyway."

"Sorry to hear it," said John. "I'll keep a look out."

"Thank you," Ralph said and turned his horse homeward. He paused. "John," he called.

John turned back, convinced his crime was discovered and he would be breaking rocks at Leavenworth before sundown.

"Yeah?" John said.

"Wait here," he said. Ralph rode off and disappeared over the hill.

John was convinced he was busted but decided to suck it up and did as he was told. The fence coil was burning a hole through the bottom of the wagon.

Ralph returned, hopped off the horse, and reached around for his saddlebag.

Expecting a gun, John hopped down to use the wagon as a shield. He peeked cautiously over the wooden tailgate.

Instead, Ralph approached with a jar of green peas and one of carrots. John's mouth fell open.

"My mom asked me to bring this over to your ma as a thank you for the chicken she brought over after Daddy lost his mama," he said. "We all sure appreciated your kindness."

John stepped down and sunk into the soil; he could smell the wire. He walked over to Ralph and reached out a hand.

The men shook hands. John said, "You have no idea what this means to my family."

"We do for each other in tough times," Ralph said. "That's what Mama says."

"She is a wonderful woman, Ralph," John said. "To tell you the truth, I'm heartbroken."

Ralph tipped his hat to shield his eyes from the sun. "What for?" he said.

John turned toward the wagon, carefully placing the jars of vegetables in the back—in case Ralph decided to renege his gift, he could still make a run for it. John grabbed the coil of wire and said, "I just picked this up over yonder. I was stealing it to try to fashion a greenhouse for some veggies. My youngest brother Lee is weak as a kitten and looks like hell."

Ralph stood looking at John. John said, "I'm sorry, Ralph. I'm ashamed of myself."

Ralph took a deep breath, and John expected fire to fly out at him.

Instead, Ralph mounted his horse, tipped his hat to John, and said, "Hell, that wire is so rusty it isn't worth stealing."

"Well, desperate times," said John.

"Keep it," said Ralph. "Let me know if you need more."

"Thank you, sir," said John. "Tell your mama thank you, too. She saved a life today."

"She thinks she saves a life every day," Ralph chuckled.

John laughed and watched Ralph disappear over the hill.

"Well, I'll be damned," John said. He put the wire back in the wagon, lifted the jars up out of the bed, and placed them safely between his legs for the ride home.

As he approached the house with Mrs. Bates's gift, Marie saw him coming and the jars glistening in the sunlight.

"Where did you get those?" asked Marie, running out to meet him.

John explained how he scored the vegetables, and Marie got to her knees right there in the middle of the yard, cradling the jars in her arms and thanking God for his kindness. She carried the jars to Lee's bedside and woke him.

Lee rubbed his eyes and sat up.

"Lee, can you hear me?" she asked.

"Yes," said Lee with a yawn.

"As God is my witness, I will load these peas in a six-shooter and fill you full if you won't eat them on your own. Am I clear?" her voice low and firm.

"Yes, ma'am," Lee said, swallowing hard.

Marie turned on her heel to take the jars into the kitchen and, Lee supposed, to clean a gun.

19

He will cover you with his pinions,
and under his wings you will find refuge;
his faithfulness is a shield and buckler.

Psalm 91:4

Fred guessed the good soil was at least four feet below the layers of dust and sand that blew in from every part of the country. The idea of digging that far into the ground for a few tomatoes seemed excessive. He and John walked around the place looking for a place for the greenhouse. They consulted Miles and he was able to make some suggestions on the construction if they left the soil in the cellar. The best dirt was down there and well protected.

"Really? We aren't gonna haul the dirt up here," said Marie.

"No, we shouldn't have to," said John. "That's probably the best dirt in the county under there, and it's shielded from storms. We can't improve on that."

"It would be easy to rebuild the cellar door with windows to get the sunshine down there," said Fred.

"But it's so chilly down there," said Marie.

"It won't be once the sun has a chance to take a peek," said Fred. "Carrots and peas like it cool."

"What choice do we have?" said John. "We have to try it, right?"

Silence touched the lips of each of them, and they knew this was the only real shot they had at growing anything for Lee.

They spent a good deal of mental energy working out the details.

As storms approached, they could cover the cellar's new window doors with the original wooden door for protection, then remove the door once the danger passed. Grasshoppers could certainly eat through repurposed wood, so it was decided that they would rotate their chickens over to a makeshift corral around the opening. As long as the chickens didn't tire of the leaping buffet, it should deter the insects from investigating what's down below. As far as jacks were concerned, Uno was the best deterrent and could stand guard with Clete or Lee to keep the critters away.

Fred suggested spreading a mixture of molasses and bran, which he had heard would get rid of the bugs. Marie didn't want to draw the ants, so she suggested a test area far away from the cellar, which was a good option to make everyone happy.

Clete offered to help Fred build the frame for the windows, and Lucy and John took Big and Shorty to town for a few supplies, such as seeds and hinges.

It was random luck that the cellar door faced south to the winter sun. Marie, Angela, and Elaine began planning their crop. They dug four short rows, only two of which would be in the direct path of the sunlight. Marie decided to place an eye hook in the center of the dirt ceiling above the rows. She tied some of the fence wire to the hook and strung it down to the ground. She hoped the peas and beans could climb up and get some sunlight from above the plant base this way. Angela used some of the cedar posts to create a base for the wires, and they were placed about every two feet along the outside rows, which were reserved for peas and beans. Broccoli and carrots were planned for the center rows. Hoping for more success, they wanted to stick with some cool-weather plants.

Clete and Fred made great progress on the frame and had it in place before John and Lucy made it back from Merna with the supplies. Once they returned, it was just a matter of putting the windows in place. John decided to build a second frame to fit about a foot below the newly windowed doorway against the bottom part of the outer windows. Fred thought the second frame, for ease of getting in and out of the garden, should be built in two pieces and open from the center out. It was a great idea and an additional barrier to keep the world out.

John was concerned about the sunlight opening being half the size of the cellar room.

"I'm not sure it can heat that much space with so little sun," he said.

"We have to try," said Marie.

John kept the problem at the front of his mind and continued trying to come up with an additional way to keep the plants warm. He decided to visit with George Eblin up the hill, who lived in a soddy. That man must have lots of ideas on staying warm.

All in all, it was a good start to an unpredictable project. Everyone came together at the dinner table that night, and the teamwork had been good for their souls. Lee sat in his usual seat, staring forlornly out the screen door at Uno, who sat on the other side, drooling and licking his lips. There wasn't a six-shooter in sight, but Lee knew his mother wasn't one to exaggerate. He chewed the peas on his plate as if they were eggs hatching lizards in his mouth. It was difficult to keep them in. The texture of the pea was a right disgusting thing. Lee was certain that God had intended the pea for cattle or goats to eat. Certainly the Lord could come up with a better flavor and color for something a young child would need so desperately. Marie sat next to Lee monitoring his spoonfuls and providing a visible check after each bite. Lee couldn't believe she could stand to see the mushed-up vegetable paste in his mouth. Each time he swallowed, she verified his success.

It was certainly more difficult to enjoy a meal this way, but he knew there would be no argument with Mom. Fred always said trying to win a battle with Marie was like feeding cherries to pigs . . . there just wasn't any reason for it.

That evening, John settled down at the kitchen table and wrote a letter to the government, inquiring about a tree belt. It was a few weeks later that an agent showed up at the door. The suited man measured and drew up what the McClouds could get approved for, but he did require that the area be fenced.

John bit his lip and tugged on his left ear, as he generally did when trying to hold his tongue.

"Why would you fence in some trees?" John asked.

"Why wouldn't you?" replied the agent.

John inhaled deeply.

"It's about a half mile of fence in all," said the agent. "You can come up with that, can't you?"

"I suppose I can," said John.

John turned the agent over to Fred for the social commentary and excused himself. He walked to the resource pile the family collected for Lee's garden. There wasn't much left. Ralph Bates said to let him know if John needed more . . . John didn't want to grovel but supposed it was in order.

John hooked Big and Shorty up to the wagon and headed out to the Bates' place. He saw Ralph in a pasture on his way there. John tried to wave at him from the field; a fence stood between them. Ralph took notice of John and his team and hopped on his horse to approach.

"Howdy," Ralph said.

"Hi there, Ralph," John said. "What ya' working on?"

"Just trying to unbury a water tank. Damn weather," Ralph said. "I'm guessing you need more wire?"

"Only if you can spare it," said John, reaching into his pocket for the agent's drawing. He explained the agent's plan and unreasonable need to have the trees fenced in.

"We got some," said Ralph. "See that corner post over there on the side of the hill?"

"Yeah," said John.

"Bring your wagon over there," Ralph said.

John snapped the reins, and Big and Shorty moved toward the corner of the pasture. Ralph rode slowly on his side of the fence. When John reached the target, he waved at Ralph. "There's no gate here," John said.

Ralph slid off his horse, dug in his saddlebag, pulled something out, and casually approached the fence line. He reached out with a pair of wire cutters and cut all three strands of wire.

"There's a gate," he said, returning to his horse.

John followed him about a quarter of a mile into a canyon. There was a stack of posts and dozens of wire rolls.

John's eyes widened as if he'd seen the promised land.

"How much do you need?" Ralph asked.

John crawled off the wagon and handed the drawing to Ralph, who opened the paper and gave it a once over.

"Looks like you'll need three rolls of wire and all but two of the posts," he said. "I'll help you load them up."

"Are you sure?" John said.

"I'm sure," he said, approaching the pile of supplies.

"I can't thank you enough," said John.

"We do for each other," he said.

"Well, it's true you have been doin' for us for quite some time," John said. "I'm not sure I've been doin' much for you, though."

Ralph laughed out loud.

"You mean your daddy never told you?" he asked.

"Told me what?" asked John.

"He saved my daddy's life," Ralph said. "When they were young. About sixteen. Daddy's horse got away from him and left him for dead in the canyon. Your daddy loaded him up and brought him home. Broken ribs and a collar bone, I believe. Had a lung collapse. He would have never made it back without your daddy's help."

John was floored. He had never imagined his dad was capable of something like that.

"I didn't know," John stammered.

"You need anything from us," said Ralph, "it's yours."

"Well, I'm glad you told me that," said John. "I appreciate your kindness, and you sure don't owe our family anything. Let's call it square."

"That's up to our daddies," Ralph said.

"Fred isn't holding it over your head is he?" John asked.

Ralph looked at John for a moment with a curious expression—not quite confused but certainly not following.

"Hell no," said Ralph. "Your daddy is a good man, John. He has his demons, that's true. You probably know that better than anyone.

A life is a life, and he saved my daddy. I will always be grateful. In fact, your daddy probably didn't tell you because he's embarrassed at how we fuss over him."

John felt shame climb into the seat next to him. "Well, I'm sorry I didn't know," said John. "I appreciate your help regardless."

The two men filled the wagon, and John steered it around to exit the freshly made gate. He hopped down to help Ralph repair it, and they shook hands to go their separate ways.

Without the help of the Bates family, John knew there would be no way of getting a shelter belt. In fact, John still had a battle to face, finding a posthole digger. He swung over to Joe Knoell's place to see if he could borrow his. As always, Joe was more than happy to help. John loaded it up and headed home.

John recruited Clete to help dig the postholes, and the two of them got to work. The goal was to have the fence done and pass inspection this fall; then they could plant the trees in the spring.

Lee sat in the Radio Flyer wagon, which was rescued from the resource pile, watching John and Clete from inside the makeshift chicken coop guarding his vegetables from grasshoppers. With a fly swatter, Lee smacked every hopper he could reach. Uno and the chicken on duty took care of the ones he couldn't reach. He had no idea how the plants were doing in the cellar but was hopeful that his condition would improve before the harvest. He had eaten more peas and carrots and potatoes than he had ever dreamed of consuming, which had never been much. The two jars only went so far in Mom's eyes, although it was already to the point of making Lee want to vomit, which everyone knew would be counterproductive.

The weary child sat basking in the warm sun, grateful for the wagon but also tired of having to use it. He missed running with Uno, seeing rattlesnake fights, and helping collect eggs. He missed the occasional ride on the back of Uncle Bill's tractor. How he loved working with that man. Uncle Bill drove the purest rows of crop he'd ever seen—like a chess board, straight in every direction. Lee hoped the garden grew foods for Mom's sake, but he dreaded the thought of eating from it.

"God," Lee said, "I don't want to undo my mom's praying. But I gotta tell you I hate eating green things. They make my stomach turn, and I don't think I can handle it much longer. Please, Lord, I know I don't want to be sickly; and I don't want to die; but I need your help. I'm not ungrateful, God. Please help me."

Uno had his fill of hoppers and lay his head in Lee's lap. The dog watched the chicken continue waging war and admired its style of pecking at the insect and stabbing it. It then used its clawed foot to pull it off the beak and ate it right up off the ground. Very efficient.

Lee stroked the dog's neck and felt a breeze pick up speed and temperature. He lifted his gaze to the north. A duster was coming.

"John," he yelled fearfully, since he wasn't able to get himself to safety. Uno stood at attention. The wind was hot, as if from the earth's stove. Uno snorted the heat out of his nose with no success.

"Dad," Lee yelled, "a duster's coming!"

He sat motionless listening for the screen door to bang or footsteps to approach. Uno began circling and whining.

"Mom," he yelled.

No one came. The wind picked up dirt and grasshoppers, and the air began clouding.

Uno wouldn't leave his side. Lee wrapped his arms around Uno, and the dog started walking. Lee fought falling out of the wagon.

Lee reached out to the chicken coop gate and managed to get the latch undone with the wire end of the swatter. The entry flew open.

"Uno," he said, "I can't walk. Get help."

As the air thickened, Lee covered his mouth with his shirttail. Uno began barking. Darkness crept up on them. The chicken cackled and cried and finally fulfilled its dream of flying.

All of a sudden, Lee fell back in the wagon and had the sensation of movement. Certain that he was to meet the chicken's fate, he latched onto the wagon side with a white-knuckled death grip.

He could hear Uno whining, but his sound seemed muffled. Lee tried to open his eyes, but the dirt blinded him as soon as his lids lifted. He was sure he was moving. The wagon bumped along and suddenly picked up speed.

Confusion overtook Lee, and he collapsed in the wagon. His fabric mask flew away from his face, and he thought, I'm gonna end up on Ray Johnson's porch.

Marie and the girls were in the house, knee-deep in locking down the windows and doors for the storm, when Fred said, "Is Clete with Lee?"

"Oh no," said Lucy. "Clete is helping John in the barn."

Marie dropped her towels and ran for the door. Fred stopped her. "I'll get him," Fred said.

Fred opened the screen door into the furious winds and pelting heat that felt as if it were cooking you from the inside. He stumbled down the porch stairs into a pile of fur.

Uno lay draped over Lee's body in the wagon.

Fred pushed Uno off and lifted Lee from the Radio Flyer. He flung Lee's limp body over his shoulder and gripped Uno's fur behind the head and carried them both up onto the porch. Marie stood at the door unable to see what was happening just feet from her eyes. She heard Fred before she saw him.

"Marie," he yelled, "take Lee."

Marie reached her arms out into the nothingness, stepped out, and found her son's backside. The girls filled in behind her to keep her tethered to the house. She sightlessly grabbed the child by feel and backed her way into the house. She laid the boy down on the couch and said, "Angela, tend to him."

She returned to the screen door and reached out for her husband. She found fur. She grabbed it, and Uno fell into the doorway atop her. Fred crawled in behind him.

Fred coughed and spit mud out. He wiped his red, watering eyes and went to Lee's side. Elaine and Lucy checked on Uno, who was still breathing but was unconscious.

"That damn dog pulled the wagon to the porch and then lay on top of him," Fred said.

Marie looked toward the dog without the ability to speak.

"John is smart enough to stay in the barn," Fred said. "We can't worry about them. John knows what he's doing, and they'll be fine."

Marie didn't know what to do other than clean Lee off. They drug him to the washroom and removed his shirt. She could see the dampened spots in the fabric where he had covered his mouth to protect himself.

"Good boy, Lee," she said.

Without another word, she bathed every corner of him. She scooped dirt from his ears, nose, and mouth and rinsed him as best she could.

They took him to the lower-level bedroom and carried Uno to his side.

The two slept for an hour before one of them stirred; to Marie's disappointment, it was Uno who woke.

~ 20 ~

We love, because He first loved us.
1 John 4:19

John and Clete tried to keep the horses and milk cows calm during the onset of the storm. They were certain Lee was fine. After all, they hollered to the house for someone to get him as they rounded up the livestock; and if no one came, Lee could have just crawled down into the cellar and sat the storm out with Uno.

"Are you sure?" said Clete.

"No," said John. "But Lee is smart, and you know that dog won't allow anything to happen to him."

"Let's go find him," said Clete.

"You stay here, Clete, where I know you're safe," said John.

"I don't want to be in here by myself," said Clete.

"Well, do you really want to be out there by yourself?" said John.

"No," said Clete, not following the logic. "We can tie ourselves together so we don't get separated."

John stood staring at the closed barn door.

"It's a good three hundred feet to the house," John surmised. "Can you make it that far? We'll get to the house; and if Lee isn't there, I'll keep moving and you stay inside."

"Deal," said Clete.

It amused John how readily Clete was to throw him back out in the storm.

"Let's find something to cover our faces," said John.

131

"What about this seed sack?" said Clete.

"Perfect," said John. He reached out, grabbed the sack, and dumped out what seed remained in the stall with the horses. He dunked the fabric bag in the water trough and wrung it out with his hands. "The wetness will hold the dirt on the outside," he said. "Come here."

Clete felt butterflies in his stomach trying to escape.

John held Clete's shoulders and squared him up to John's face.

"We are gonna make it," John said. "If we don't, Mama is gonna kill one or both of us. Do you got it?"

"Yes, John," Clete said.

"It's just three hundred feet, Clete. We can walk it in our sleep," John said.

Clete nodded, trying to project confidence.

"Okay, I'm gonna put this over your head and tuck it into your shirt collar," John explained. "Then I'm gonna tie us together at the waist with Big's lead rope. We will crawl on our bellies to the house."

"What is going over your head?" Clete asked.

"I'll find something," said John. "Don't worry."

John tied the rope around Clete's waist, stringing it through a couple of his belt loops. He then placed the sack over Clete's head, noticing a tear falling on Clete's cheek. Unsure of what to say to soothe the boy's fear, he simply tucked the bag into his collar and said, "Okay, Clete . . . just stay there . . . I'm gonna cover my face now."

The burlap form nodded. John tied the rope around his waist and pulled his shirt up around his nose, covering his chin and mouth.

"Are you ready?" John said. "It will go faster than you think. When we step outside, just squat on the ground while I get the door closed and latched. When I tug on the rope, we move."

"Okay," the bag said.

"Take a good deep breath, Clete," John said.

The sack figure grew an inch or two and then relaxed again.

"We go," said John, opening the barn door.

Clete stepped out into the deafening blizzard and sunk to the ground. John pushed the barn door closed, which took a lot more effort than he had planned. He knew now that this wasn't a typical dust storm. This was something different. The air was so hot it felt like he was standing on the sun. The barn door latched easily enough once he got it closed. He knelt down and took hold of the rope, keeping his feet pushed up against the barn door to use it as a guide to project his line. He tugged on the rope and felt Clete begin moving.

John started on his hands and knees and quickly realized that he needed to belly crawl. He reached out for Clete and pulled the bagged boy closer and reached up to his backside and pushed him down. Clete stayed low, reaching out to John. The two figures snaked their way through the yard. The dirt stung every part of their exposed skin. The air roared with hate, and John couldn't help but think it sounded evil.

Clete began to feel claustrophobic in his seed bag and John sensed panic was setting in with his little brother, and he needed to quell that quickly.

He could feel Clete's energy wane . . . he sensed the boy was losing his will. John crawled slower, and the kid couldn't seem to keep up. Finally, John felt Clete stop completely. The boy dug into the ground and wanted to sit it out. John had no idea how much farther the house was but knew now this was a bad idea.

John felt his way under Clete's belly and found a hand. He grabbed it and squeezed hard. John refused to stop moving—to stop was to die . . . maybe not today, maybe not in the yard, but certainly within a month, tucked in bed with mud leaking out your nose. That wasn't gonna happen to them. John wouldn't stand for it.

Another terrible idea struck, and John went with it. He got up on a knee, leaned over Clete's frame, and picked him up. John forced himself to stand and continued moving forward . . . he was pretty sure he was going in the right direction. The slope of the land felt familiar, and he followed his instincts.

Clete curled up in a ball and swung an arm around John's neck. They moved this way for some time and seemed to be making some progress, but even Clete could tell that John was losing his strength. John was breathing as best he could, but the buttons on his collar slipped open and began allowing a wind tunnel of dust into his mouth. Clete placed his bagged head in front of John's face. He didn't know if it would help, but it certainly couldn't hurt. He knew John had no line of sight to the house anyway.

John focused his mind on Lee, on if he was safe, on how he was gonna do this again if Lee weren't in the house. He decided he would be better served thinking about fried chicken. That sounded good. He guessed a few of the hens wouldn't survive the storm and that meant good eating.

John crashed into a wall and found the porch railing. He followed it with his hands to the steps and fell forward with Clete rolling and thumping into the screen door. Clete reached up and found the handle just as the wooden door opened from the inside. Fred stood towering over them, and John heard someone reach for Clete.

John knew it was Fred by the sound of his boots. He also knew Fred would love to leave John out in the storm, but the joke was on Fred. . . John was tied to Clete. John kept his eyes closed and felt his body being drug into the house.

"What the hell are you doing taking Clete out in this?" Fred yelled.

"Is Lee here?" John spat, coughing up at least one lung.

"Yes, John," Marie said. "Uno brought him to the door."

"Is that why you did this," said Fred, "to check on Lee?"

"Well, I wouldn't do it for kicks," said John.

"Just rest, John," Marie said. "Elaine, can you bring John a washrag and something to wash his mouth out with? John, you rinse and spit in the sink a few times."

Clete sat on the couch clutching his seed sack and looking at John. "Are you okay, John?" he asked.

John smiled at Clete, "What did you want . . . to build a fort out there?"

Clete laughed.

Marie kneeled down next to John and waved Clete over. Clete sat on her lap and wrapped his arms around her neck. Marie leaned forward to place her forehead on John's shoulder.

"Thank you, John," she whispered.

Fred stared down at them without knowing what to say. He was mad as hell at John and couldn't figure out why everyone trusted him so much. He could have killed Clete. Why wouldn't John think Fred would take care of Lee? Fred was the one who had asked about him, wasn't he? Fred was the one who drug him inside, wasn't he? Where was Fred's teary-eyed thank you? He turned his back to all three of them and walked into the kitchen and sat down at the table, staring in at the bed that still cradled Lee. He could hear the kid breathing but couldn't figure out why he hadn't woken up yet.

Uno raised his head and turned to look at Fred. The dog was worried too—Fred could see it in him. The dog nestled his head into Lee's armpit and licked his cheek a couple of times. Fred could hear Uno take a deep breath and whine as he exhaled. If he didn't know better, he'd have thought the dog was crying.

By the time John felt like standing up, the winds were subsiding. He stood brushing himself off in the foyer. He removed his boots and jacket and shook himself a few times to try to get out the loose dirt particles. He moved down the hall into the kitchen and stood looking into his parents' bedroom at Lee and Uno. He entered the room to sit on the bed and give Uno a good rubdown.

"You're a good dog, Uno," he said. "A damn good dog."

"Language," Marie said from the kitchen.

John winked at Uno. Uno sat up and walked toward Lee's feet. The boy's toes were bare and hanging out from beneath the blanket. Uno licked one foot and it kicked. The dog licked it again and Lee murmured, "Uno, stop."

"Lee," said John. "Wake up, Lee."

The whole house gathered in the doorway of the room. Lee opened his eyes, cleared his throat, and looked around the room with surprise.

"What's the matter?" Lee asked.

Everyone laughed with relief, and the tension went by way of the dust.

"Praise God," said Marie. She walked over to the bed and tousled Lee's hair. "What would we ever do without Uno?"

Fred fumed.

"How do you feel?" she asked.

"Good," Lee said; but the moment the word was out, his face changed. He heaved a couple of times. Uncertain of what was happening to him, he finally turned his head away from the bed, vomiting peas and mud and, to his horror, a grasshopper onto the floor.

John laughed. "Don't worry Lee; I may be next." John turned to find Fred sitting at the kitchen table glaring as if he could kill him just by thinking it.

John stood looking at him for a moment. He pulled up a chair sitting across from Fred.

"Something on your mind, Fred?" John said.

Fred sat quietly, "Nope."

"Well, you let me know if you ever want to chat," said John.

"Will do," Fred said.

"Alright then," he said. "Ma, I think we need to celebrate Lee's return."

"Good idea," said Lucy, and the girls got busy in the kitchen to pull together some food.

Marie turned to see John and Fred eyeing each other. She stood appraising them and then shut the bedroom door. She stayed in the bedroom with Lee for a few minutes and then came out with some soiled, smelly towels. She handed some to Fred and some to John.

"Would you boys be so kind as to help me out," she said. "Why don't you rinse these out in the washroom."

The men went from looking at each other to looking at Marie. "Really?" said John.

"Really," said Marie. "I believe I've made myself clear to you both."

Fred stood and took his linens to the washroom, closing the door as he entered.

John whispered to Marie, "I didn't start it."

"Neither did I," said Marie. "I refuse to live with it."

"Maybe Fred needs a refresher from that Bible," John said.

"We all do," said Marie. "John, when you're done with your washing, please get the Bible and pick out a few verses for our reading tonight."

John sunk.

Marie returned to the bedroom with a glass of water for Lee.

John turned to see how Lee was recovering and to thank him for his extra chore. And that's when it hit him. No one covered the cellar door.

"Shit," John said.

"Language," Marie said.

"We didn't cover the cellar," he said.

Everyone sunk.

"It's in God's hands now," Marie said.

Lee's heart sang praise, and only Uno could sense his sudden improvement in mood.

21

He humbled you, causing you to hunger
and then feeding you with manna,
which neither you nor your ancestors had known,
to teach you that man does not live on bread alone
but on every word that comes from the mouth of the LORD.

Deuteronomy 8:3

The morning following the storm was spent cleaning and sweeping and coughing. Fred, John, and Clete worked in the cellar, trying to unbury the seedlings that had emerged over the last few weeks. It was not a job for impatient men. Three inches of dirt needed to be dusted off the plants without pulling the fragile roots from the ground. The dirt was loaded in a milk bucket, which Clete carried up to ground level and added to one of the drifts laying against the house.

The windows were broken and would need to be replaced. It was the first time the men really had a good look at the garden, and each of them was impressed with how warm it was in the hole and how green the saplings looked against the dark, rich soil. It reminded them what life was like in the good times, and whether or not a crop was harvested . . . they were inspired by the experience.

"Maybe we should water these plants with holy water," Fred said.

"Don't give Marie the idea," said John. "I have enough on my plate."

Fred sat back on his heels, "Your plate?"

John looked up. "Our plate," he said.

Silence filled the room.

"You know, John," Fred said, "you are doing a good job with the place. I wish you would acknowledge the work that was done before you were put in charge."

Unwilling to comment, John continued working in the soil. He tugged at his ear and bit his lip.

"I know you're disappointed in me," Fred said. "But I ain't always been sickly. I had dreams and ambitions, but life has a way of changing things . . . not always for the better."

John tasted blood.

"When you get to be my age with ailments and children and bills to pay," Fred said, "you may look back and see me differently."

John paused, sat back on his heels, and took a deep breath.

"Fred," he said, "Ralph Bates told me about what you did for his daddy years back. To tell you the truth, I'm still not sure I believe it. I don't know the man who would spend a little bit of extra effort to help someone in need. I have grown up watching you sit in that porch chair, complaining about the way things are and doing nothing to change any of it."

Fred sunk.

"I wish I knew the man who saved Ralph's daddy. I can respect him. And you don't have to tell me life is hard. Look around. Who doesn't have a hard life? I'll be leaving this farm as soon as I'm old enough, and I suggest you and Marie move to Merna. If you can't handle the work . . . if Clete wants a different life and this place won't make it long enough to give Lee a chance . . . Wake up, Fred," John said. "Your life is leaving you behind."

John stood up and brushed the dirt from his knees. He turned to ascend the cellar stairs and passed Clete coming down with an empty bucket.

He heard Fred say, "Good job, Clete. You're really working hard, aren't ya?"

John pulled himself to the barn, fighting the urge to turn around and give Fred a little bit more of his thoughts. He knew he'd already said too much and that Marie would be on him. John wasn't worried about being asked to leave, though; Marie still needed him. Miles was doing a good job, but rumor had it that his girlfriend was pregnant, which couldn't be good news for the McCloud family. Next year, John would worry. For now, he would just walk it off.

As John passed the porch, he found Lee and Uno sitting on the front steps.

"Well, there's a sight for sore eyes," he said.

"Hi, John," Lee said.

Uno approached John for a head scratch and returned to Lee's side.

"How are you feeling?" John asked.

"Better," Lee said. "Just tired."

"Well, you got to start eating something," John said. "I know you hate to hear it, but I think your garden is gonna make it just fine."

Lee's face soured. "We'll see," Lee said.

John tousled the boy's hair. "Do you want to come to the barn with me?" John asked.

"Na," Lee said. "Elaine and Lucy are looking for my wagon. They thought it may have blown down the lane."

"Who knows," John said. "If they can't find it, I can dig up a wheelbarrow for you."

"Thanks," Lee said.

John turned toward the barn. Three steps in, he heard Lee say, "I bet you could fit in the wheelbarrow with me, Uno."

John turned around as he continued walking backward up the yard, "The goal, Lee, is to walk again on your own. Don't you teach that dog to put his feet up, too."

Lee smiled, "Uno works hard you know."

John said, "That's because he eats so many vegetables."

Lee scrunched his nose up and shook his head back and forth.

John disappeared into the barn. Lee wrapped Uno up in his bony arms and lay his head on Uno's shoulders.

"You're a good dog, Uno," Lee said. "Thanks for saving me."

Uno licked Lee's shoulder and worked his way up the neck to his cheek. When Lee felt Uno's tongue pull at his nostril, Lee drew the line there. "That's enough, Uno."

Life returned to normal, or as normal as it had ever been without much food, rain, or milk. For some reason, the chickens seemed to fare well, and the eggs were plentiful. The storm thinned out the grasshoppers and jackrabbits; and other than the drifts of dirt everywhere, it seemed like any other beautiful Nebraska day, with blue skies and puffy white clouds. Lee leaned back against the steps and soaked it all in. He wished he could go help John or ride on the back of Uncle Bill's tractor. It was probably silly to think Bill's tractor was working, given all of this dirt; but the experience replayed in Lee's mind. He imagined the crisp, cool morning air while discing the clay soil. He felt as if he were riding waves in a boat as he clung to the back of that tractor. He learned to keep his knees loose, which let him go with the flow without injury.

Elaine and Lucy walked up the lane, pulling the Radio Flyer wagon. It didn't seem to be damaged other than the fact that the handle wasn't as straight as it used to be. Lee smiled at their approach.

"Here you go, buddy," Elaine said. "Wanna go for a ride?"

"Yeah," said Lee. "Can we go see if Uncle Bill is discing?"

"Oh boy, that's a long ride," said Elaine.

"How 'bout we go see if John can take you over on Midge or Big?" suggested Lucy.

"That would be great," said Lee.

The threesome walked and rolled to the barn with Uno in tow. John was more than happy to comply. He always enjoyed Uncle Bill's company and needed to get as far away from Fred as he could to cool off.

"Who should we take?" asked John.

"Midge," Lee said. "I miss her."

"She misses you," John said, as he reached for her blanket. "Do you want a saddle, or should we risk bodily harm?"

"Bodily harm," Lee said smiling.

"Blanket it is," said John, reaching for Lee. He lifted the child up and almost swallowed his tongue at the shock of how light the boy had become. The boy was wafer thin, and John decided Uno covered him up in the storm to literally keep him from blowing away.

Lee scootched up on the blanket, and John hopped up behind him.

"Lucy," John said. "Tell Ma we'll be back."

"Will do," she said. "Have fun."

The girls waved the pair down the lane; and when they were out of sight, Elaine broke down into tears.

"Did you see how light he is?" she asked.

"I know," Lucy said. "God help that boy—he's starving himself to death."

Lucy wrapped an arm around Elaine and started walking her to the house. "Don't let Mama see you crying over Lee," she said.

Elaine took a deep breath and wiped the tears from her face. "He's fine," she said. "He will be fine as soon as that garden grows."

"Amen," said Lucy.

John and Lee rode quickly over to Uncle Bill's place, and Uno had a hard time keeping up. He always showed up though so Lee wasn't worried. Lee cherished feeling the cool breeze brush through his hair. He felt normal again to be galloping through the hills; atop Midge, it didn't matter if he couldn't walk. He wondered if he would be strong enough to spend any time on the tractor. John could tell Lee was enjoying the ride, and so he took a detour to show him where the old Dutchman's windmill used to stand. Lee laughed as John explained which parts of the windmill were now holding his garden frame together. Uno trotted up about the time they were ready to go again.

They let the dog catch his breath and then eased the horse across the prairie.

"I love it here," said Lee.

"I do too," said John. "It's a lot more fun with rain, though, isn't it?"

"Yeah," Lee said. "But it's still God's country. Every breeze is a breath of heaven."

John smiled, having heard his mother use that phrase more than once.

"Feels a little bit more like hell's panting at the door lately, though, doesn't it?" asked John.

"Maybe sometimes," said Lee, smiling.

They could see Uncle Bill's homestead in the distance. Lee was restless, and John was excited to have a visit too. It seemed as if the whole area was left a wasteland by yesterday's storm. Drifts lay everywhere. Fence lines were buried. Tumbleweeds made their way across the nothingness.

"Uncle Bill," Lee said from atop Midge, waving frantically at the man.

"Well, hi ho there, slick," Bill said. "How the hell are ya', son?"

"I'm good," said Lee.

John slid off the back of Midge.

"Well, come on down here, lad," Bill said. "I'm just about to take the tractor for a spin."

Lee lit up and looked toward John. John reached up for Lee and lifted him down, holding him on his hip like an infant.

Bill's face wrinkled and squinted. Lee's smile about broke the bank, and John looked disappointed that he hadn't thought this through . . . He should have given Bill some warning about Lee's situation.

"Polio?" asked Bill.

"Picky eater," said John. "He's wasting away."

"Lee," said Bill. "Slick, you've got to eat, son."

"I know, sir," Lee said. "Can we ride the tractor first?"

Bill shrugged, "Can you stand?"

"For a little while," said Lee.

"Alright then. John, bring him over," said Bill.

John carried the child, who felt like a handkerchief in his hand. He placed Lee's feet on the belt pulley near the rear axle, and Lee pulled himself up to the back of the seat. Uncle Bill climbed aboard; and if John didn't know better, life "looked" normal. Lee was smiling from ear to ear, and Uncle Bill was working at something other than survival.

"Try this, Lee," said John, removing his belt. He fitted it around Lee's butt and strung it through the eye of the rear of the tractor seat. "That'll give you some help." Lee grinned as he sat back into the makeshift bench.

"You can go on inside and listen to the radio," said Bill.

144

"Radio?" said John. "When did you get that?"

"When Fred bought me out of the land," said Bill. "I almost have a hard time listening to it 'cause the guilt of it grabs at me, but we all make our own choices."

"Fred makes a lot of bad ones," said John.

"He's a good man, John," Bill said. "If God would cooperate, you'd be a millionaire by now."

"Ha," John said. "Have a good ride, Lee."

"Bye, John," Lee beamed.

John knocked on the front door and let himself in. Aunt Ruby was sitting in a chair by the radio, embroidering on God knows what. John had always feared that if he sat still long enough in her presence, he would be stitched in place. She sewed constantly. She didn't enjoy cooking, which John guessed was fortunate during these lean times.

"Hi, Ruby," said John. "Lee needed a tractor ride from Uncle Bill."

"Oh, how is that boy?" she asked. "We miss him so."

"He's struggling, ma'am," said John. "Needs to eat more veggies. He's starving himself and letting that dog of his clean up. In fact, Uno came with us. He'll be rolling up the lane pretty soon."

"Oh, how frightful," Ruby said. "Take a seat, John. Can I get you anything?"

"No," John said. "I'll just rest a spell while they spin their wheels a bit."

"That's fine," said Ruby. "The president is on now talking about some of his new programs. God, help that man save our country."

"We're getting a shelter belt in the spring," said John.

"Is that right?" Ruby asked. "Wonderful."

The president's voice boomed out of the wooden box, and Ruby and John leaned toward the sound.

"I am certain that the people of this country understand and approve the broad purposes behind these new governmental policies relating to agriculture and industry and transportation. Within the umbrella of the Agricultural Adjustment Act, we have created the Federal Surplus Relief Corporation, which will help us deal with the excess supply of crops, which resulted when prices fell dramatically. To support farmers and families, the federal government will buy basic farm commodities at discount prices and distribute them among hunger relief agencies in states and local communities."

"What does that mean for us?" said John.

"Fruit, John," Ruby said. "His examples earlier were Florida's oranges or Washington's apples. They are having booming crops, and no one can afford to buy them to eat . . . So instead of letting them waste away, the government will buy them and distribute them to those of us who need food."

John smiled and stood up. "Thank you, Aunt Ruby," he said. "I have to go."

"But you just arrived," she said.

"Lee is killing himself by not eating vegetables . . . Maybe he will eat fruit," said John. "I have to get to town to figure out where to apply."

"Oh, that's magnificent, John," she said.

"Can Lee stay here while I go?" John asked. "I'll be a lot quicker without him."

"Of course," she said. "Take as long as you need."

"Thank you, Ruby," John said. "Thank you."

John missed every step jumping off the porch and leapt up on Midge. He wished now he had a saddle, but he could ride at a pretty good pace on a blanket.

Uno started as John kicked his heels into Midge's side. John could tell the dog was considering following him, so he hollered, "Uno, stay."

The dog was more than happy to comply, and a cloud of dust flew up in the air around his full furry frame as he plopped down into the dirt.

John didn't know where he could get any information but had heard his dad talking at church about the library regarding the loan program. He decided that was a good place to start.

~ 22 ~

For I was hungry and you gave me something to eat,
I was thirsty and you gave me something to drink,
I was a stranger and you invited me in, I needed clothes and you clothed me,
I was sick and you looked after me, I was in prison and you came to visit me.
Matthew 25:35–36

By the time the first crate of oranges, peaches, and apples arrived at the McClouds' door, Lee's garden was starting to develop. The carrots were coming along more quickly than the other plants, and it was obvious to everyone that Lee had been eating them by the orange tint to his skin, fingernails, and eyes. His body and mind were desperate for some variety. Even with an occasional jar of canned vegetables or fruits from the Eblins, Aunt Ruby, and Mrs. Bates, Lee's body was having a hard time accepting food. He was almost always nauseous and could only eat small bits at a time without heaving it up onto the floor.

Marie peeled the first orange, and the scent of sunshine filled the room. She decided it may be easier for Lee to drink the juice rather than eat the solid meat of it. She squeezed it by hand into a small glass and took it into his room.

"Lee," she said. "Try some of this wonderful orange juice. Fresh from the groves of Florida."

Lee looked at the glass, "It's orange."

"Well, of course it's orange," Marie said.

"I don't want to be orange anymore," said Lee.

"No arguing," she said. "Drink."

147

Lee leaned up on one elbow, and Marie held the glass to his lips. As the scent found Lee's nostrils, he pulled back from the glass.

"Please try," said Marie.

Lee leaned into the glass and inhaled a bit of the citrus flavor. "It smells strong," he said.

"It will make you strong," she said.

Uno fidgeted at the foot of the bed. Lee looked over at his dog and could tell that Uno was worried for him. The dog had a way of holding his ears that let Lee know that he was supposed to be doing as his mama said.

Marie held the glass closer to Lee, "Please."

Lee reached out and grabbed the glass. He closed his eyes and laid the cup against his lips. He couldn't decide if he should sip or gulp. He decided to sip until he knew the juice wouldn't make him vomit.

Marie watched the boy's hands tremble as he drew the cup to his lips.

Finally, he swallowed a sprinkle of the juice and licked his lips. "It's good," Lee said.

"Of course it's good," Marie said. "Now how do you feel? You will need to drink it slowly. Your stomach is touchy, so don't overdo it."

Uno's tail wagged heavily against the mattress . . . thunk, thunk, thunk, thunk.

Uncertain if his stomach would rebel, Lee drank some more. Thunk, thunk, thunk, thunk.

"I like it," he said. "It seems to like me, too."

"Thank God," said Marie. "Now don't you worry about being orange; it will go away as we get you back on your feet. Besides, it's always been my favorite color."

Lee smiled. Thunk, thunk, thunk, thunk.

Lee drank three small glasses of juice that day and ate one full apple.

Marie worked furiously in the kitchen canning half of the apples and peaches so that they wouldn't spoil. It was all for Lee she decided. No one else could have any until Lee was on his feet. It wasn't a popular decision; but as long as she could can it, there was no worry of it going to waste. She was more liberal with the oranges, since she didn't

148

think they would keep in a jar, and it may do all of them some good.

Clete carried the jars of fruit down to the cellar. It always surprised him how warm it was in there. He placed the jars on the shelves and returned to the house.

"Ma," Clete said, "is it too warm down there for the jars?"

Marie stood upright. "Oh, it may be. Good thinking, Clete. Let's find another spot for them."

Clete turned on his heel to retrieve the booty.

Marie convened with Fred and John on the porch.

"Where can we store the jars where they will stay cool and still be handy," she said.

John thought quietly. Fred said, "I know."

"Clete, come with me," he said.

Clete loaded the jars in the Radio Flyer wagon and followed Fred to the barn. Fred got Midge ready to ride, and Clete filled the saddlebags with jars.

"You want to come?" Fred asked Clete.

"Sure," said Clete, and Fred lowered his arm toward him. He grabbed Fred's hand and pulled himself up. It was always easier to get on if no one was already in the saddle, so it took him a minute to get situated.

Fred clicked his tongue, and Midge moved forward at the sound. They approached the porch.

"There's a cave about a quarter mile west of us, where an old moonshiner used to hide his hooch. It will be a good spot, and no one outside of our family and the Eblins know about it. The shiner is long gone. We'll be back soon."

Marie nodded and smiled, waving the boys off.

Fred steered Midge up to the ridge of the valley and stopped by George Eblin's place.

"Clete, wait here," he said.

"What are we doing?" Clete asked.

"I'm just letting George know what we're up to since the cave is on his land now," Fred said.

"Oh," said Clete, and he wrapped Midge's rein around his knuckles.

Fred approached the door, knocked, and waited for Liz Eblin to greet him. She directed Fred to the field behind the house, where George was working. Fred tipped his hat to Liz and almost tripped on a chicken making its way into the soddy.

He reached down to stop it from entering the house. Liz reached for his arms, stopping him.

"Oh that's Penny," she said. "She lays an egg on my pillow every day like clockwork. We don't mind her coming in."

Clete laughed in his head at the whole scenario, wondering what his mom would do if a chicken tried to lay an egg on her pillow.

The chicken hopped over a sleeping dog who lay in the sunlight of the open door. Before Fred was back on the horse, the chicken came out with a look of relief on her small beaked face.

"Well, I'll be," Fred said quietly to Clete and tipped his hat toward Liz. He clicked his mouth and Midge moved. Fred directed her to the field behind the house, and they found George skinning an animal.

"Hi there, George," said Fred.

"Well hello, Fred," he said. "Hi there, boy."

Clete suspected the man couldn't remember which son he was but said nothing.

"We're gonna put some canned goods in that old moonshiner's cave up yonder," Fred said. "We've put a garden in the cellar, and so it is a bit too warm for the jars to keep."

George stood straight. "A garden," he said. "Really, well now, I would like to see that. Are you getting anything?"

"Lots of carrots . . . some peas . . ." Fred said.

"What a great idea," said George. "Impressive, Fred. Impressive."

"And how is that sickly boy," he asked. "Better?"

"We hope so," said Fred. "Just got some fruit from the government, so we'll see if it builds him up."

"Good news," he said. "You know, Fred, there is a great deal of protein in grasshoppers. I know it sounds awful, but if it comes to it . . . why the hell not?"

"I'll remember that," said Fred. Fred could feel Clete trying to keep his laughter in.

"Well, be careful in that cave," said George. "I haven't been there for some time. Who knows what may be calling it home these days."

"Thank you, George," said Fred. "We will watch ourselves."

Fred clicked Midge to a start, and the pair continued to the cave. Clete was anxious to see this place and couldn't believe how much fun a boy could have in such a place. His imagination was spinning circles around them.

Fred approached the side of a hill that was tucked in behind some cedar trees. He hopped down from Midge and held the reins to steady her as Clete climbed down. Fred pulled three jars out of the saddlebag and handed them to Clete. Fred carried the other three jars.

"Okay," Fred said. "It's gonna be dark in there. I'll go in and you can hand me the jars from the outside. There may be snakes in there, so you're staying out."

Clete sunk. "Yes, sir," he said.

Fred brushed back a tall patch of grass and started kicking the hill. Clete thought he may have lost his mind but on the third kick the earth fell inward exposing a hole. The dark mouth was about two feet wide and about one and a half feet tall. Fred lay down on the ground with his feet facing the opening.

"I don't know why, but I'd rather go feet first," he said. "Wish me luck."

Clete stood holding the three jars, wondering what he would do if Dad got bit by a snake.

Fred squirmed as he slid into the hill. Clete saw his head vanish into the darkness, it was as if he were swallowed up by the earth.

"Okay, Clete, hand me your jars," Fred said from the void.

Clete reached in with one jar at a time.

"Are you sure a critter won't get these?" said Clete.

"Nope," Fred said.

When all six jars were lined up along the wall, Fred's head emerged as quickly as it had disappeared. Clete backed out of the way as Fred pulled himself out, stood, and brushed himself off. He found a fallen cedar branch and pulled it over the opening of the cave and approached Midge.

"Mama's waiting on us," he said.

Clete grabbed Fred's extended hand and pulled himself up to Midge's saddle.

"Let's bring a lamp next time we come," said Fred. "I'll show you around in there. We used to play in it as kids."

"What's it like?" Clete asked.

"Two big rooms," Fred said. "Rumor has it a man named Kelly dug 'em out. He was a miner turned moonshiner. No one knows what happened to him. Here one day, gone the next. He left behind a bunch of jars of food, booze, and who knows what. They are probably still in there, although I'm sure it's all rotten."

"Wow," Clete said.

Midge trotted all the way home.

As they were getting off the horse in the barn, Clete asked, "Can you really eat grasshoppers?"

Fred laughed. "Clete, you can eat anything you want," he said. "I'm gonna stick to Mama's cooking, if you don't mind. George is probably right, though. He's a smart man, and he has studied a lot of different things. But it's your choice if you want to eat a grasshopper."

Clete laughed. "No thanks," he said.

Fred and Clete worked together to remove the riding gear from Midge, and Clete walked her back to her stall.

─ 23 ─

Trust in the LORD and do good;
dwell in the land and enjoy safe pasture.
Psalm 37:3

Fred started renting out the back pasture to Ray Johnson for his stock to graze. Ray paid forty cents per head per month. The cattle were there for four summer months. The annual income from those four hundred acres was ninety-six dollars. Fred agreed to furnish the salt, water, and related costs. He also promised John would handle the fence upkeep and weekly inspections. All these arrangements were made without any discussions with Marie or John.

John was furious when he found Ray's cattle eating up the only good land left for McCloud milk cows and livestock to graze. It was also apparent that the windmill was no longer pumping water, even though it seemed to be running. John discovered a rod had parted inside the well. This repair was above John's ability, so he called in a plumber from Merna. John would have preferred to use the plumber in Anselmo, but Fred wouldn't allow it because he was a protestant. For ninety dollars the Catholic plumber fixed the windmill; and after the cost of the salt and other expenses were taken into account, Ray Johnson owed Fred six dollars.

Marie encouraged Fred to raise the fee to fifty cents.

Fred said, "No, Ray will take his cattle somewhere else."

John said, "Let him; we need that land."

After much heated discussion, Marie put her foot down. She said,

"Fred McCloud, if you don't charge that man fifty cents per head, then you will need to move into that cave up the hill. If Ray takes his cattle somewhere else, he'll pay a hell of a lot more than that."

Fred stared at Marie, pushing his lips outward then pulling them back in. It was his way of saying, "The hell with you," without having to speak a word.

Marie crossed her arms and pursed her lips. "Shall I get your coat?"

Fred turned and walked outside.

John said, "Thank God you have some sense. And another thing, Ray is lying about the number of head he keeps out there. I've been counting, and he has seventy-two out there. He's only agreed to sixty."

"Let's wait and see what his payment is on the first of September," Marie said. "Maybe he will add the additional money on."

"You know he won't," said John.

"Hush," said Marie. "Ray is your father's friend."

"Friend my ass," said John.

"Language," said Marie.

John tugged at his ear.

"Not another word until September 1," she said.

John nodded.

Lee and Clete were upstairs in the bedroom and could hear all of the commotion downstairs. Uno lay uninterested in front of the window, soaking in the sunlight.

"Do you think Dad will go live in the cave?" asked Lee.

"No," Clete said. "Mom is just better at math than Dad."

"Oh," said Lee.

Uno sighed, weary of the boys' chatter.

Clete asked, "How are you feeling today?"

"Good," said Lee. "I want to go outside. Do you think Mama will let me?"

"Sure," said Clete. "Let's go."

Clete stood, presenting a hand down to Lee, who grabbed it with both of his hands and pulled himself to a stand. As he stood, his pants fell a bit.

"Here," said Clete, handing him a belt from the dresser.

Lee took it and strung it through the loops on his pants.

"You look like a scarecrow," said Clete.

"Thanks," said Lee. "At least I'm a walking scarecrow."

Clete laughed, "And you're not orange anymore."

The pair carefully descended the stairs and found Marie at the bottom.

"Well, look at you today," she said to Lee. "You are looking like a million bucks."

Lee couldn't imagine what that looked like, so he just smiled. Uno stood at the top of the stairs pushing his back toward his tail and leaning into a nice stretch. The dog waited for the boys to reach the bottom before he yawned and hopped down step by step. He brushed up against Clete's leg at the bottom and placed his head below Lee's hand. Lee petted the dog's neck without a word.

"Can I go outside today?" Lee asked.

"Absolutely," she said. "Do you think you can make it to the chicken coop?"

Lee beamed. "Yes, ma'am."

"Great," she said. "Can you and Clete go look for some eggs for me?"

"Yes, ma'am," Lee said.

Marie kissed Lee's forehead and said, "I'll be right back with the basket."

Clete pushed the screen door open, and Lee stepped forward. The sun warmed Lee's toes first and then scaled up his body as he reentered the world.

Marie came up behind him with the basket, handing it to Clete.

"Don't leave him," she said to Clete.

"Yes, ma'am," Clete said.

"Have fun," she said.

"Thanks Mom," Lee said.

Uno stepped off the porch and wandered into the center of the yard, which was becoming a busy place. John had applied for and received a AAA loan from the government, with which he had bought four horses, a Hereford bull named FDR, and some additional milk cows. The bull was a great addition, because with some planning, the McClouds could have milk all year long. In the past, arrangements had been made with the neighbors to borrow a bull in the hopes of romance to keep the cows lactating. It always seemed like each of them calved at once, which meant they all dried up at the same time. Now romance had moved in, and love called month after month.

Lee walked toward the chicken house with Uno and Clete on either side of him.

"I miss this," said Lee.

"Keep eating," said Clete. "I miss it too."

The boys found two eggs in the chicken house but figured there were more to be found in the horse barn. It was becoming a favorite place for the chickens to lay their eggs. The hay mow had holes in the floor so hay could be tossed down into the horse stalls. In each side of the front of the stall was a box for the horses to eat their oats out of; under these boxes was where the chickens liked to lay their eggs. The tricky part was reaching your hand in blindly to feel for the egg.

"You first," said Clete. "You miss this, remember?"

Lee laughed. "You big wimp."

Lee lay down in front of the box, letting his hair brush up against the stray bits of straw sticking out of the floor boards. The musty scent of urine and soil mixed in his nostrils, and he inhaled it deeply. With one arm braced up against the stall door and one arm reaching underneath the end of the hay box, Lee fingered his way around the darkness. He found one egg and retrieved it.

"I think there is another one," said Lee.

He resumed his position and put his arm back inside the box. His fingers felt the egg, and he tried to wrap it in his hand to pull it out. However, a bull snake had the same idea and had already gotten its mouth around the other side of the egg. When Lee tried to grip the egg, he grabbed the snake's head.

Lee pulled his hand back like a lightning strike and gasped.

"What?" said Clete.

"Bull snake," said Lee.

"Really?" said Clete.

"You put your hand in there," said Lee.

"No thanks," said Clete laughing. "Those are harmless."

Uno sniffed the hay box.

"Well, it scared me out of a year's growth," said Lee.

Clete laughed. "Do you need to piss?"

"I already did," said Lee. "Just kidding," as he pointed out the dryness of his pants.

Clete laughed, and the boys finished their egg hunt, finding eight.

By the time the chore was finished, Lee felt like he'd walked ten miles; but he knew it was good exercise and that the bull snake was nothing more than a good heart check.

It was great seeing life on the farm again. The new horses and cows and crops made the place feel like home. The grasshoppers subsided, and Lee believed credit was due Uno for that achievement. The jackrabbits had learned to keep a distance from the house, and so, all in all, life was back to normal. Marie seemed to be back to worrying about rattlesnakes, and even that felt right.

Lee didn't know much about politics, but he knew the shelter belt, the loan for the animals, and the fruit were saving lives, including his. The bull named FDR was a small tribute to a great man . . . Lee even appreciated the bull's dedication to the ladies. Life was good, and it felt like it was only going to get better.

He will be like a tree firmly planted by streams of water,
Which yields its fruit in its season
And its leaf does not wither;
And in whatever he does, he prospers.
Psalm 1:3

Miles was doing a great job. The disc bearing on the lister froze up, and the bolts that held the bearings were too big for any of the wrenches Miles could find in the shop. The hired man asked Claude for the use of a wrench that would work, and he took it all apart, repacked the bearings, and put it back together. The rumor about the McClouds' treasured workman would turn out to be true. Miles was going to be a father. It's a shame that when he returned the wrench to Claude, no one heard from him again. Miles broke many hearts that day, John's included.

It was time to start discing, and John had Big and Shorty hooked up in the center with the two new young horses on either side of them. John hoped the younger ones would learn from the older ones and that the next generation of workhorse would be ready for Clete when he took over.

Clete was busy milking, and John was really feeling productive, moving along the field in the early morning—one of John's favorite times . . . before the heat of the day crept up on you and the grasshoppers realized you were out of bed.

John was settling in for a full day of work when a pheasant flew up alongside the horses. Startled, they took off running. John tried to pull them in, but the lines broke. He lost all control and couldn't decide if he should hold on or jump off. Having a runaway with a disc on board was about the worst scenario he could imagine. Discs were known to twist from side to side and eventually flip forward, crushing the driver and clipping the heels of the horses, causing usually mortal injuries to all. He decided to ride it out and white knuckled the seat while he was being thrown and tossed around; he could feel his back getting jarred at every jolt. Finally, he determined he couldn't hold on any longer. John bailed out to the side, trying to get enough ground between himself and the disc coming up behind him. The machinery caught his boot and tore it clean off, leaving his sock in place. He didn't feel so much as a tickle, which seemed impossible, but he lay on the hard, cracked soil watching his boot dance after the horses.

The team ran about a mile and stopped. John caught up to them and unhooked the disc as soon as it was within reach. Scooping up his boot, he moved to grab Big's bridle. The horse gave John the evil eye and threw spit at him. Shorty was digging his hooves down into the ground, letting John know he was finished for the day. The young horses were shaking and trying to figure out what just happened. Each of them fidgeted in place, shaking their heads up and down.

John let the foursome calm down for a few minutes and strung the broken rein through each of their bridles. He pulled them together toward the house and left the disc where it lay. He leaned on Big's shoulder to put his boot back on and then walked the team back to the barn. He unhooked them all and Clete and Lee helped brush them out. Brushing was one thing that usually made them happy and required very little effort, so it was worth the time.

Lunchtime arrived, and virtually nothing had been accomplished. John, Clete, and Lee walked toward the house to eat, when they noticed a crew of eleven men walking up the lane, carrying shovels and hoes. The men were followed by a wagon full of saplings.

"Well, I'll be damned," said John. "The shelter belt is here."

John walked through the yard to meet them.

"Well, hello," said John.

"Hi there," said a man with clean hands. John guessed he was the manager of the bunch.

"I'm Daniel with the Civilian Conservation Corps," he said. "Are you John McCloud?"

"In the flesh," said John.

"We're here to plant some trees for you."

"Perfect day for it," said John. "Do you fellows need to eat, or are you ready to work?"

"We're ready," said Daniel.

"Well then, follow me," John said, walking the men toward the fenced area he and Clete had prepared last fall.

"This looks great," Daniel said. "What we plan on doing is eight rows of trees, five different species for about one-eighth of a mile."

"Sounds great," said John.

"When we're finished," Daniel said. "I'll come up to the house with some information on how to care for the trees so they grow straight and tall and fill in appropriately."

"Looking forward to it," said John. "Is there anything I can get for you?"

"No," said Daniel. "We carry everything we need with us."

"Well, have at it," said John.

Daniel tipped his hat at John and then turned to his men. The group looked to be each less than thirty years old, and all dressed in matching pin-striped overalls. The shirts they wore were from their own collection and looked to be the only thing they had owned and worn for a good deal of time. Some of their sleeves were shredded. Some of them rolled the sleeves up to hide missing buttons. All of them were filthy. John admired these men. He tipped his hat to them and said to no one in particular, "I want to thank you men on behalf of my family for your work here," he said. "It means a lot to us, and if no one else has said it to you, I will . . . you are making a difference in this God-forsaken world. Thank you."

The men seemed appreciative, but none of them spoke. All of them tipped their heads toward John to acknowledge him, and John guessed they were under instructions not to consort with the locals. They were all very dirty, so it was clear they had been working hard for quite some time. Manual labor has a way of leaving its mark on a person.

Clete and Lee watched from the lane.

John approached them. "What a crew," said John.

"I thought we would have to plant them." said Lee.

"Nope," said John. "Putting people to work is the point, I guess. That FDR is a pretty good egg."

Lee said, "I was looking forward to working on that. I figured I would be strong enough to help by then."

"Well, today is your lucky day, Lee," said John.

Lee looked at John cautiously, "Why?"

"You can be the man in charge of taking care of those trees. You'll need to weed them and water them and I don't know what else. That man Daniel is going to come up to the house to teach us what to do," said John. "Daniel said they are planting eight rows of five different species," said John. "That ought to make it interesting, Lee. And they're only going one-eighth of a mile. Thanks for volunteering."

John patted Lee's boney shoulder and headed up the lane.

Lee's mouth fell open.

Clete said, "I'll help you, Lee."

They all turned back toward the house to get the lunch they set out for earlier.

It didn't take Daniel long to find his way up to the house. Lee met him on the porch.

"Are you Daniel?" Lee asked.

"Yes, I am," Daniel said. "And whom might you be?"

"Lee," the boy said. "I'm in charge of the trees."

"Well now, you have your hands full," said Daniel. "But don't worry. They are each pretty hardy breeds."

John came to the door. "How did it go, Daniel?" he asked.

"Great," Daniel said. "I think you'll be happy."

"We're thrilled," said John. "Come on in."

"Thank you," said Daniel. The man followed John and Lee in the house and down the long hallway toward the kitchen. Fred got up from the kitchen table and offered Daniel his chair.

"Thank you, sir," said Daniel. "I'm Daniel with the CCC."

"Fred McCloud," said Fred. "Thank you for your work."

"It's our job, sir," Daniel said modestly.

Daniel sat in Fred's chair. "Now Lee tells me he's in charge of the trees. Is that true?"

"He volunteered," said John.

Lee sat meekly, knowing there was no way out. Fred smiled at Lee some encouragement.

"We'll all help out," said Fred.

John tugged at his ear.

Daniel spent a good deal of time describing the different species of trees and their individual strengths and weaknesses. For the most part, each species was fairly drought resistant and hardy. However, keeping the weeds out and watering when able was recommended. He laid down a best-case scenario of how much and how often and warned them against overwatering. Everyone barked with laughter, and Daniel didn't seem to understand why. The agent recommended that the length of the belt be divided up by days of the week and that each day, Lee focus on that segment of trees to care for.

"That will give you a consistent amount of work to figure in with the rest of your chores," Daniel said. "It shouldn't take more than a couple of hours a day. The better you keep up with it, the easier each day will be."

"Do you have any questions?" Daniel asked.

"Nope," said John. "Can we go down there with you for a tour?"

"Sure," said Daniel. "Let's go."

Fred, Lee, Clete, and John followed Daniel down the hall.

Fred wielded his gift of gab and kept Daniel talking for the trip to the shelter belt. The CCC laborers gathered in the shade of a cedar tree at the end of the lane. Until this morning, it had been the only tree within a half mile.

It was beautiful. The trees were planted in perfect rows, equally spaced and freshly watered. Fred was impressed. John came jogging up behind them. Marie followed, although no one realized it yet.

Daniel reviewed the species of each row and explained why they were planted in that particular order.

John decided Daniel really liked to hear his own voice.

Marie walked past her family, crossed the lane, and approached the workers in the shade.

"Hi there," she said.

The men tipped their hats.

One of them whispered, "Ma'am, we're not supposed to talk."

Marie tilted her head. "Well, if that isn't silly . . . Wait right here."

She turned to approach Daniel.

Fred saw her approach and introduced her.

"Pleased to meet you, ma'am," Daniel said.

"Daniel, where are you and the boys staying tonight?" she asked.

"In Anselmo," he said. "The Catholic church has agreed to host us while we work in the area."

"Well, Daniel, today is Monday. And I imagine you may not be aware that today is my wash day," she said.

Daniel attempted to say something, and Marie spoke over him.

"Now, I just will not tolerate these hardworking men being dressed in these filthy clothes. So, what I'm gonna do for them is wash those shirts overnight and return them to the Catholic church by morning."

"Well, I appreciate that, ma'am," Daniel said. "But that won't be necessary."

"I notice you say that from a freshly pressed shirt," Marie said. "It is necessary, and I won't take no for an answer."

"I'll send John along with you to your next stop, and he can return the shirts to me here. When your workday is finished, I will wash them and return them to the church by morning."

"Well, we start really early in the morning," he said. "I appreciate . . ."

John tugged his ear. Fred bit his lip. Marie continued, "I can have them to you by 3:00 a.m. Is that early enough?"

Lee could see the men were interested in what Marie was trying to do for them, and he could see them fidgeting and whispering. Lee loved this side of his mother. She was such a caring person, and no one and nothing was going to keep her from doing what she felt was right. He could see his dad and John were embarrassed about it, but Lee was proud. He stood taller watching her do things like this.

"I can go get the shirts, Ma," Lee said, "if John has work to do."

Marie looked at Lee, "Are you sure you're ready?"

"Yes, ma'am," Lee said. "I can ride Midge and take Uno."

Daniel knew he had lost. "Fine, ma'am," he said. "The men will appreciate your kindness."

"Thank you, Daniel," Marie said. "Lee, let's get you ready."

Marie turned with her arm around Lee and walked slowly back toward the house.

John didn't know what to say, so he said nothing.

Fred said, "Welcome to McCloud Valley, Daniel. Where the men don't argue."

Daniel laughed. "She is a kindhearted woman, but I wouldn't want to make her mad."

"Now we understand each other," said Fred. "Thank you for allowing her this gesture."

"Our pleasure," he said.

The men in the shade smiled and looked forward to the treat of a clean shirt by morning.

The McCloud place wasn't the first stop the tree crew made that day. They had already planted a shelter belt at the Bates' place. After they finished the McCloud farm, they were off to Ray Johnson's house to surround him with trees. John read in the newspaper about a month later that all of the trees in the Nebraska Reforestation Project were planted by hand. The best eleven-man crews could plant between five thousand and six thousand trees in an eight-hour day in previously cultivated earth. Of the 18,599 miles of trees planted nationwide, Nebraska received over four thousand tree-lined miles, more than any other state. The belts varied in length, from one-eighth of a mile to a mile, and averaged about ten rows of trees, containing between five and eight different species. The total cost of the program was almost $14 million, of which almost 90 percent was paid to farmers affected by the drought, mostly for their labor on the planting crews.

— 25 —

He has made every thing beautiful in his time. . . .
Ecclesiastes 3:11

John was starting to think about leaving. He was old enough to find work and certainly knew how to take care of himself. He had been putting his money in the Merna bank for a few years and felt a little bit like a Rockefeller. He sold a couple of cattle and decided his time had come. He wandered over to the used car lot, and a salesman who didn't seem to be too excited about John's ability to make a purchase approached him.

"Looking for a car?" he asked.

"Yes, sir," said John.

"What can you afford?" he asked.

"Forty-five dollars," said John.

He stood looking at his shoes for a minute and then said, "Wait here."

John stood admiring the shiny vehicles parked all around him, knowing that none of them were in his price range.

The salesman came back and said, "There's one out back you can look at."

He pointed to a 1931 Ford sedan sitting all alone in the back. He made no move to show John the car—just pointed at it and said, "Go take a look."

John walked toward the car thinking it may be his lucky day. About thirty feet from the car John was certain he had stepped in dog shit.

The smell was everywhere. He checked his shoes, coming up empty. It was then he realized—it was the car. He moved upwind and peeked in the car. The front seat was pristine. The body was good. The backseat, however, was missing. In its place was a layer of straw and about two inches of dog shit.

Taking a deep breath, John slid into the driver's seat, where he found the keys already in the ignition. He started it up. It purred. He drove it around the back lot and decided it was his.

He brought it around to the main lot and parked. The salesman came over, standing upwind from the car.

John said, "I'll give you forty-five dollars for it if you will get me a back seat."

"There's a wrecked '30 over there; you can take the back seat out of it."

"Then you've got a deal," said John. "My money is still in the Merna bank."

"Bring it in next Saturday," he said. "I'll draw up the papers while you get your back seat."

"Deal," said John.

It was easier than John expected to remove the back seat from the wrecked car, and he tied it to the top of his new car. The salesman came out with the papers and dropped them in the front seat of the car. He didn't hang around to visit with or congratulate John.

He was reluctant to ask about the car's history but knew it would haunt him if he didn't.

"So," John said, getting the salesman's attention, "how did it end up this way?"

"Ha," the salesman barked. "A never-been-married hunter thought it was a great place to keep his hunting dogs."

Tilting his head, John took a minute to absorb the idea.

"Hmm," John said. "Well, his bad idea is now my gain and at a good price."

"I'm glad you are happy with it," said the salesman. "See you Saturday."

John nodded and eased the car out onto the road. It was an odd situation, although John felt proud driving it home, stench and all.

As the car turned in the lane and approached the house, John could see Lee and Clete working in the trees. They waved and ran alongside him. Uno trotted along with them, excited at the chance to stretch his legs.

John couldn't help but laugh when he noticed the smell hit them. Both boys slowed to a crawl, rubbing their noses and checking their shoes for manure. Uno was the only one who kept up in the wake of his smelly chariot.

John pulled the car into the barn and opened the doors to air it out. At least, he thought, when Marie takes a look at the car, it won't be as obvious how stinky his purchase was. It was hidden among the odors of the other animals.

John began shoveling out the crap from the back and tossing it in the wagon. Fertilizer is fertilizer.

Clete and Lee approached with smiles glistening from ear to ear.

"Wow," said Lee. "What a great car."

"How much was it?" asked Clete.

"Never you mind," said John.

The three of them worked together to clean up the car and install the back seat. It became one of John's favorite memories of his brothers. It was the one time John could remember working with them on something that was completely free of Fred's involvement or commentary. The boys were certainly different personalities with unique strengths, hopes, and dreams. But in this one afternoon, they had a common purpose, which they all wanted equally. It was beautiful, dog shit and all.

By the time Marie came down to the barn to see the car, the back seat was installed, most of the elbow grease was spent, and John had sworn the boys to secrecy of its previous condition.

"Would you like to go for a ride?" asked John.

"Sure," said Marie.

"Can we go?" asked Lee.

"Hop in," said John.

Everyone fit comfortably. Marie sat in the front seat with John while Clete and Lee occupied the back. Uno, the only one truly not offended by the stench, tailed along behind.

As they turned out of the lane, Marie said, "You shouldn't have parked it in the barn; now it smells a little like poop."

John said, "I wasn't thinking, I guess."

John glanced in the rearview mirror at Lee, who smiled at their shared secret.

They took the car up the road past Ray Johnson's house, down through the Bates' property, and then back up through McCloud Valley.

As they came up the lane, Marie said, "I'm proud of you, John."

John turned to her smiling. "I'm proud of me, too."

Marie swatted his shoulder and turned to the back seat, "Which one of you boys is gonna run the farm when John leaves us?"

Clete and Lee sat speechless.

The car rode silently back into the barn. "John, don't park it in here," Marie said. "The smell . . ."

"A little smell never hurt anything," said John.

Fred stood on the porch watching the car turn in. He entered the house without a word or gesture of interest in John's purchase. He hoped the appearance of the car meant John might be leaving soon.

The awkward silence following Marie's question told her everything she needed to know. It was time to move to town.

— 26 —

The joyriders entered the house to find Fred oiling the mantle clock and the Edison phonograph. He used a feather and kerosene and immense concentration for this task. The tension in the room rose three notches as Fred looked over his shoulder, glaring at the group for interrupting his focus.

John didn't have the patience to accommodate Fred's need for silence and announced he was going to the barn. Clete and Lee followed his lead.

"We'll bring in the milk cows," said Clete.

"Thanks," said John.

Lee chose Midge and Clete mounted Bugle, one of the new horses John had brought in. They clicked their heels into the horses' sides, and off they went into the pasture. They were riding south into the wind. Lee tired of having the wind in his face and decided he would have a better time riding Midge backward so as not to face the cold wind.

"That's not a good idea," said Clete.

"I'm fine," said Lee. "She's smooth. Riding backward is easy."

"I know she's an easy ride, but that doesn't mean it's a smart idea," said Clete.

Determined that he had solved his problem, Lee didn't alter his position.

All the way out to the cattle, things went as planned; then as

Clete rounded the milk cows back toward home, one of the younger cows decided to make a break for it. Midge, on instinct, went after the cow, leaping into a gallop. Lee fell hard on the frozen ground and knocked the wind out of his chest. He had fallen directly in the path of the remaining milk cows, and he was barely able to stand as they brushed past him. When the last cow rounded him, his lanky frame collapsed to the ground desperate for air. He could feel himself panicking and knew Clete had gone after Midge and the cow.

Fear gripped him, and then he had the thought of Clete telling him, "I told you that wasn't a good idea."

Lee gasped, staring up at the stars. He could see he was breathing because his breath was clouding up in front of his face. He focused on the North Star, trying to calm his nerves.

He heard Bugle's hooves approaching.

"You alright?" asked Clete.

"Yeah," said Lee in a whisper.

Bugle whinnied as if having a good laugh. Midge walked up to Lee and nudged his face with her snout.

Lee grabbed her bridle. "I'm fine Midge," he said. "It's not your fault."

"What did I say earlier?" said Clete.

"I know," said Lee. "Let's just drop it."

Midge laid her neck over Lee's shoulder and turned her head in for a hug. Lee wrapped his tiny arm around her and patted her neck. Weaving his fingers into the horse's mane, he launched up to her back and clicked his tongue twice. Midge started forward, and they caught up with the cattle already trotting down the curved clay path toward home.

"Don't tell anybody," said Lee.

"Why?" said Clete. "We all take our spills."

"I don't know," Lee said. "I just don't want everyone worrying about me again."

"Okay," said Clete. "But if you start feeling you broke something, you tell me."

"I will," said Lee, knowing he had broken nothing but his pride.

John met the cattle at the gate and waited to let them through it until the cowboys rode up.

"Where you been?" asked John.

"Bugle is a bit fidgety," said Clete. "We're fine."

John swung the gate open, and the horsemen rode through guiding the cattle toward the barn. Uno met the cows at the front of the building, turning them into the barn doors.

Each of them took notice of the new car parked in the middle of their home. It was probably John's imagination, but he swore he caught a few of them checking their hooves for manure.

The boys put the cattle in their stalls and pulled down the buckets and benches for milking. Clete and Lee got started, and John put the horses away.

After the milking was done, the boys each carried two buckets of milk over to the cream separator. It had a crank handle to turn that John would get started, and then they would take turns without stopping the crank. It was a challenge to keep it going during shift changes and required a good bit of timing. But if it stopped, it was a bear to get going again, so everyone understood the importance of doing it right.

"I'm gonna take a shower," said John.

"Okay," said Clete. "We got it."

"I'll be right outside if you need me," said John.

"Okay," said Lee, watching Uno lick the empty buckets clean.

John had built a shower coming directly out of the supply tank, which was a really nice feature. Most of the time the water was pretty cold, since it was heated only by the sun. It had been a sunny day, though you could see your breath; John guessed the water would feel pretty good. He had layers of the day to remove.

Clete and Lee heard John squeal, "Wow, that's cold."

John guessed wrong; but once wet, he was committed. He scrubbed and breathed in deep, trying to adjust to the temperature of the water.

Clete thought it would be funny to hide John's towel. Lee wanted no part of it.

Clete crept up to the door, quietly lifting the towel from it. He ran.

Lee cranked the separator, trying to see where Clete would go with the towel.

"This is not a good idea," said Lee, leaning toward the open side door.

Clete cackled in the moonlight. "Shush," he said.

The water stopped. Lee listened. John spat, "Where's my towel?"

"Hey," John said. "It's cold out here. Bring me that towel."

Lee feverishly worked the crank. After a moment of silence, the door flew open, and John stood naked as a jaybird dripping wet. "Where's my towel?" he said.

"I don't know," said Lee.

"CLEEEEEETE," John yelled, running out into the darkness.

Lee was desperate to see what was happening but didn't want to stop the crank until the job was done. He would need John to get it going again, and something told him John wasn't in the mood.

Uno went to the doorframe, and his head moved from side to side as if watching a tennis match. Lee watched the dog's head move, imagining the fun of what was happening.

"Thank God I took no part in this, Uno," Lee said. "John is gonna kill him."

Clete sped through the yard, dangling the towel in the darkness. John ran as if he were on fire, dangling something of his own.

The chase lasted longer than Lee expected. He couldn't believe John would run naked for so long in such cold air. Of course, he knew John wasn't the type to give up or cry uncle. This may have been one of Clete's more costly mistakes as John doesn't forget easily either.

Lee and Uno walked toward the house, where a crowd had gathered on the porch. An audience . . . that was why this was lasting so long. Clete was running out of breath and tossed the towel into the air. To his dismay, John had run himself dry and no longer needed the towel. He batted it down from the air and ran right over it.

Clete picked up the pace, realizing he woke a sleeping lion.

Fred smiled. Marie fretted, "John, you are gonna catch your death."

Lee and Uno sat on the porch steps. The boy smiled enjoying the chase, grateful he hadn't gotten involved.

Clete and John disappeared into the barn. Marie stepped off the porch to go find them. Clete stood on top of John's car (another poor choice), and John had him by the legs, pulling him down.

Marie stood in the barn door.

"John," she said, "let go of him."

John turned her way but decidedly did not let go. Lee and Uno walked up behind Marie.

"Clete," she said. "Apologize."

"I'm sorry, John," he said. "I was just kidding."

"Now, Clete," said Marie, "I want you to take that towel from the yard and scrub every inch of John's car. Inside and out. Do you hear me?"

Clete sank. "Tonight?"

"Tonight," Marie said.

"Yes, ma'am," Clete said.

John smiled, realizing finally that he was still naked.

"John," said Marie. "Put some clothes on."

"Yes, ma'am," said John, slapping Clete on the back of the head as he stepped away.

Marie turned back toward the house, and Lee and Uno stood watching Clete slide down the windshield of the car. As Clete's feet touched ground, he lifted his gaze to Lee.

"That was a bad idea," said Lee.

Clete rubbed the back of his head and went to fetch the thrown towel.

John put his pants on and walked across the yard. He passed Fred still standing on the porch.

"That was quite a show," said Fred.

"Well, he's lucky Marie showed up," said John.

"I'm sure he is," said Fred.

John entered the house, and the screen door bounced in the frame. He, Lee, and Uno were tucked in bed warm and tight by the time Clete crawled in between them.

"You stink," said John.

"Deal with it," said Clete.

Uno hopped down from the bed and found a spot behind the wood-stove in the dining room.

"Ugh," said Lee. "You do stink. Uno smells better."

"Go sleep somewhere else," said John.

Clete pulled himself out of bed and found a spot on the couch. He knew in the morning Marie would have him cleaning the smell out of the couch too but decided sleep was more important than curbing her anger.

Another bad choice.

— 27 —

"Clete," Marie said. "Get up. Get in that washroom and scrub every inch."

"Right now?" asked Clete.

"Right now," said Marie.

Clete yawned and began pushing himself up off the couch. It was then he knew the gravity of his situation. He must have stepped in manure while running from John. It speckled his pants and the back of his shirt, and he transferred it to the couch fabric.

"Can't believe you would sleep in those clothes," said Marie.

"Me either," said Clete. "I guess after being in that car so long I couldn't smell anything but poop anymore."

Marie raised her hand to her forehead, rubbing her brow, "I'm not going to ask what you mean by that."

Clete stood and noticed he had an audience. Uno sat staring at him from behind the woodstove. The dog seemed to feel sorry for Clete, and yet he could sense the dog was also grateful that he wasn't the one dragging smells in from the barn this time.

Clete reached down and patted Uno's head on the way by.

The washroom door closed, and Clete got to work. After scrubbing the car and cranking the separator, he felt like he had been scrubbing barnacles off the Mayflower. His arms ached, making his efforts to get clean seem monumental.

From behind the door, he could hear the house waking up and pairs of feet moving through the rooms and hallways.

Clete left the washroom as immaculate as he could. He folded and hung the dampened towel he used.

He opened the door and entered the kitchen to find the rest of his family sitting at the breakfast table.

"We're about to say grace, Clete," said Marie.

Clete took his seat and bowed his head. He could feel John's icy stare.

"Bless us, O Lord, and these thy gifts, which we are about to receive from thy bounty through Christ our Lord. Amen," said Fred.

Everyone came to life at the sound of amen.

"Good morning," Marie said to no one in particular.

"Morning," said everyone.

"What's on the agenda today?" Marie asked.

"I have papers to grade," said Angela.

"I'm going to town to apply for that nanny position," said Elaine.

"I thought I'd ride along with Elaine," said Lucy. "I haven't been to town in a while."

Clete sat stirring his scrambled eggs with his fork.

"I'll go with you girls," said Fred. "I've got some catching up to do with the boys at the general store."

"Well, that makes four of us," said Marie. "I want to visit with Doc Stone about a few things."

Everyone stopped chewing and turned to her with concern.

"I'm fine," she said. "Just getting old."

"Beats the alternative," said John.

"That it does," said Fred. "Clete, you're being awfully quiet. What are you up to today?"

Clete laughed. "Cleaning the couch I imagine. Finishing up John's car and hoping that my big brother will forgive me for my prank last night. I didn't realize how cold it was until I was out in it awhile. I'm sorry, John."

"Apology accepted," said John. "But I'd shower with a towel on your head from now on."

"That's good advice," said Clete. "Thank you."

"No one asked what I'm doing today," said Lee. Everyone turned his way.

"I'm sorry, Lee," said Marie. "What are you doing?"

"Weeding the trees," he said slapping his fork onto a pile of eggs and toast. "The same thing I've been doing all year."

"Now, son," Fred said. "We each have our chores."

"I know," said Lee. "It's just a big job that never feels like it gets done."

"I bet you're right, Lee," said Fred. "That can wear on a person."

"How about you do the milking today, and I'll do the trees," said John. "I could use a change of scenery."

"Oh, that would be great," Lee said. "Can I?"

"Of course," said Marie. "You just listen to John's instructions."

"Thank you, John," said Lee, glancing back to Uno, who had been allowed back in the house during mealtimes. "You're a cow dog today, Uno."

Uno tilted his head to one side and let his tongue hang out as he panted approval.

The morning's tension went out with the eggshells, and each McCloud got busy with his or her day. John escorted Lee and Uno to the barn and gave Lee a rundown of which cow kicks and which ones require a special touch. Besides being incredibly excited at the opportunity for a change of pace, Lee was thrilled when John said, "Now, can you show me your tree technique?"

Lee felt ten feet tall. "Sure," he said. "It's easy—just boring."

"Farming is anything but boring, Lee," John said. "Where have you been? The world's raining grasshoppers for God's sake . . . you've raised the entertainment bar pretty high."

"I know," said Lee. "There are just some jobs that you do well just for the sake of doing them well. Not because anyone cares about them."

"Now, hold on, Lee," John said, grabbing his shoulders and turning the kid to face him. "How you do a job that you think no one cares about says a lot about who you are. Weeding those trees is very important to everyone in this family. Not only that . . . whoever lives on this land in a hundred years is gonna say . . . by God whoever cared for these trees did a helluva job. Thank God we got a windbreak to hold the ground down . . . Don't ever think what you do doesn't matter or more importantly that how you do it doesn't matter. It always matters to more people than you know. You be proud of those trees. Those trees are part of your legacy."

Lee stared at John wondering where he got this brilliant piece of wisdom. The youngest had never heard Fred speak this way. What John said made perfect sense. It shed a different light on his trees.

Sometimes Lee was amazed at John. Usually he was a straight shooter who didn't bother with dramatic descriptions or analogies. In a pinch, John always seemed to have the right words.

"I never thought of it that way," said Lee.

They collected Lee's wheelbarrow full of supplies and walked toward the shelter belt section with Uno prancing alongside. As they arrived at the section of trees that was up for maintenance, Lee said, "Let's work on it together, and then I'll help you milk after."

"Attaboy Lee," John said. "Now, show me your magic."

Lee explained what his system had been to make sure that each tree had what it needed. He regularly checked for weeds, disease, insects, and moisture. He measured the first tree nearest the road in each section to monitor the growth rate. He wrote the numbers down in a notebook. For some reason, he thought if there were a problem showing up in one section versus others, it would be earlier discovered and easier to solve. He shared his data with John, who was impressed the boy had thought to do any type of tracking.

"I'm proud of you," said John. "You really are a great kid doing a bang-up job here. Thank God you learned how to eat."

Lee smiled, "Thanks, John."

They measured the tree and wrote the numbers in the journal, and John spent a few minutes looking back at the notes Lee had made about each section of trees.

"Where did you get this idea?" asked John.

"That guy Daniel had a journal that he showed me they use at the state parks," said Lee. "They tracked more factors, but I didn't think I needed that much."

John tousled Lee's hair. "Okay," said John. "You get that row, and I'll follow in the row behind you."

"Okay," said Lee. "Oh, look at these. I love these tumble bugs."

Lee pointed down to the ground, and John leaned in on one knee. The little insects were working at a fever pitch to push little balls of manure along with their hind legs.

"I think they must need the poop for winter," said John.

"They are hard workers," said Lee. "Usually they keep me company out here. And they don't steal much of my fertilizer, so I let them be."

"Well, I'm your company today," said John. "Let's get to it."

The brothers worked on the trees for the rest of the morning and finished up a little bit before lunch. John pushed the wheelbarrow back to the barn with Lee riding inside of it covered in garden equipment.

The cows were bellowing by the time they arrived, and John decided he couldn't take the time for lunch until milking was finished.

"I'll help," said Lee.

"Are you sure?" said John. "You worked hard; aren't you hungry?"

"No hungrier than you," said Lee. "Besides, the work goes quicker with help, and then we both eat sooner."

"Okay then," said John. "You take that stall, and I'll do this one. Let's keep in touch about where we're headed in case one of 'em isn't in the mood for a strange man's hands. Some ladies get that way you know."

Lee laughed even though he wasn't sure what John meant.

The place was quiet with everyone gone to town and Angela tucked away in her room grading papers. The rhythm of the milk streaming into the pails was relaxing, even though it could be a lot of work getting it there. John was right—some cows were easier than others. Uno lay in a bit of hay at the entrance of Lee's stall. John commented on the dog's ability to sleep anywhere under any circumstances.

"He works hard, too," said Lee. "It isn't easy keeping up with me."

181

John laughed, "I believe that. Especially since you ditched that damned wagon."

Lee laughed, "You know I still don't like vegetables."

"Well, you keep eating 'em," said John. "You still need to put some meat on those bones."

"Are you fattening me up for market?" said Lee.

"Hell," said John, "we couldn't give you away 'cause that damn dog would be part of the deal."

"Awww," said Lee. "Poor Uno. He's a good dog."

"Well, nobody's selling anybody," said John.

Squirt, squirt, squirt. The milk hit the side of the bucket and raced down the side.

"So do you think you'll want to take over the farm one of these days?" asked John.

"I don't know," said Lee. "I'm not sure I'm farm material."

"What do you mean?" said John.

"Well, I enjoy farming with Uncle Bill, and I love that tractor of his. I don't mind getting dirty or working hard. I just don't know if I have the instinct to run a farm. It doesn't seem to be easy these days."

"Spoken like an old timer," said John. "It's not easy. I'll tell you exactly what I told Clete. You set your sights on what you want out of life and don't get trapped here doing Fred's job like I did. If it weren't for you kids, I would've left already."

Lee stopped squeezing the cow's teat and sat upright on his stool.

"Where will you go?" asked Lee.

"I don't know yet," said John. "The sugar factory in Geneva maybe. That's just another part of farming, though, harvesting the beets for the mill to process. I feel like there's something else I need to be doing."

"You should do whatever you want," said Lee.

"Should I?" said John.

"Yes," said Lee. "It's your legacy."

John leaned back on his stool and looked at Lee, who was smiling from ear to ear.

"Are you making fun of my speech?" said John.

"No," said Lee. "It was good. Maybe your best speech yet. It's just if I have a legacy, then you do too. You should make it what you want it to be."

John laughed. "Well alright," said John. "Thanks for working with me today. We should do this more often."

"Anytime," said Lee.

Uno got up and walked over to one of the full buckets of milk. He took a couple of licks off the top and then returned to his perch.

By the time the milking was done, it was early afternoon, and John and Lee didn't know what to do with themselves.

"Let's go for a ride in your car," said Lee.

"Yeah," said John. "Okay."

They trotted off to the barn and hopped in.

"You really shouldn't park it in here," said Lee.

"But it covers the smell," said John.

"It'll never air out in shitty air," said Lee.

"Well, look who's making speeches now," said John.

"I'm just saying," Lee said.

"I know, you're right," said John. "Where should we go?"

"Surprise me," said Lee.

John eased the car out of the barn and turned it down the lane. Uno trotted along beside them until he reached the road crossing, where he sat in a comfortable pile of brush.

The young men roared down the road. Lee rolled down his window and stuck his head out into the wind.

"Don't fall out now," said John. "Marie would kill me."

"I won't," said Lee.

John pulled the wheel slightly but sharply to the left. Lee's weight shifted, and he grabbed the door frame of the car hard.

"Nice," said Lee.

"Just keeping you awake," said John.

They ended up in Merna and found Marie and Fred standing outside Doc Stone's place. John could tell from a distance that they were arguing, and he was wishing they hadn't come to town to be a part of whatever was brewing.

"I don't need it," said Marie. "It's a ridiculous prescription."

"It's what the Doctor ordered," said Fred. "You are going to take it."

Marie huffed away from Fred and walked across the street toward the Model T.

John and Lee pulled up beside the car, "Everything okay, Mama?" Lee asked.

"I just need a new doctor, that's all," said Marie. "What are you boys doing here?"

"Just a joy ride," said John, beaming from the driver's seat.

"You be careful," Marie said. "It's not a toy."

"I'm aware, Marie," said John. "But thank you for your vote of confidence."

Fred walked in front of John's car and weaved between the door and the Model T to get inside his vehicle. He paused and stood between the cars.

"Hi, Lee," Fred said, tipping his hat to John.

"Hi, Dad," said Lee. "We finished early—isn't that great?"

"It is," said Fred. "Are you going for a treat?"

"No," said Lee smiling. "I'm watching my figure."

"Well, it won't be blowing away on my watch, young man," Marie snapped.

Fred leaned into the passenger side of John's car and said, "Doc prescribed whiskey for her heart, and she ain't takin' it too well."

John laughed. Lee didn't know what to do.

"Do you mind going by Uncle Bob's to pick up a bottle?" asked Fred, handing John a piece of paper with Doc Stone's signature.

"We would appreciate not having to take Marie into a place of immoral character to purchase the medicine for what ails her," said Fred.

"Well, that's putting it nicely," said Marie. "The nerve . . ."

"Sure," said John. "You don't mind Lee coming, do you?"

"No," said Fred, calmly shaking his head.

Marie shot from the Model T, "Of course we do. Lee, come get in our car. We're going home."

"Awwww, Mom," said Lee.

"Right now," she said.

"It's okay, Lee," John said. "I'll take you for a ride another day. Thanks for your help."

"Okay," said Lee, reaching for the door handle and walking around the Model T to sit with his mother.

Fred said, "You need money?"

"Yeah," said John. "My money's in this car and at the bank."

Fred dipped four fingers in his front shirt pocket and pulled out some bills, passing them across the seat to John. "This should be enough. Thanks for sparing me the experience."

"Sure," said John. "I'll tell Uncle Bob hi,"

"You do that," said Fred nodding.

John moved the car forward waving the money at his mother, knowing it would get her Irish ruffled up. Lee waved, and Fred opened the door to enter the Model T. John turned the corner to head out to Uncle Bob's house to retrieve the medicine requested.

John was impressed by Bob's operation. He had one son in charge of the money, another in charge of the delivery, while Bob himself seemed to supervise quality. John met his cousin Morris at the barn door and handed him the slip of paper.

"One dollar," he said.

John handed him the bill without getting a receipt.

"Do I need the prescription back?" asked John.

"Na," he said, pointing him toward the garden.

Another cousin approached John and shook his hand. He pulled a paper sack out of his overalls and walked down the row of cabbage. He knelt down and picked a cabbage, which was in no way near ripe. In the same movement, he slipped a pint of whiskey in the paper sack.

"Thank you for the cabbage," said John, enjoying being part of the scheme.

"My pleasure," said his cousin smiling.

John got back in his car and headed for home. Turning into the lane, he decided that he was going to pour Marie her first glass. "Hell," he said to himself, "I'll drink one with her."

Are not five sparrows sold for two pennies?
And not one of them is forgotten before God.
Luke 12:6

John pulled into the barn to find Big, the oldest draft horse, up on his front legs but unable to pull his back legs from the ground. The horse was seventy-five in human years and had been a true workhorse all his life. He had survived the worst of the depression and had never come up sick. John knew this was serious as soon as he approached the stall. Big whinnied and muffled his lips, trying to pull himself up. His back legs were motionless. The horse spun in circles trying to muster the strength to force his lifeless legs to a stand.

Shorty, his lifelong companion and friend, watched helplessly from the next stall. He lovingly encouraged Big to keep trying. Big fell to his side and sat up. Shorty reached down with his muzzle, and they bumped noses.

John felt a tear welling up in his eye. He entered the stall and felt Big's legs and back. Nothing seemed to be painful for Big; his legs just weren't working. John didn't think anything could be broken but knew this was one injury that Big wouldn't be able to survive.

Without thinking, John went to the house to tell Fred.

"Something's wrong with Big," said John. "It looks bad. We need to call the doc."

"For a horse?" Fred said.

"He's a good horse," said John. "He shouldn't have to suffer."

"I'm not paying for a doctor to look at an old horse," Fred said. "We can put him out of his misery if it's time for it."

"But we don't have a gun," said John. "I can ride over to Joe Knoell's place and borrow one."

"We don't have time for that," said Fred.

"Big doesn't seem to be suffering, Fred," John said. "We have all the time in the world until he has some pain."

Fred walked down to the barn to find Big's predicament just as dire as John described.

Shorty looked pleadingly at Fred for help for his friend.

Fred entered the stall and knelt down next to Big.

"You've been a good horse, Big," Fred said. "I'm sorry it's gotta end this way."

John walked into the barn and saw Fred stand up with something in his hand. John figured Fred was going to kill Big but didn't think it was going to happen immediately. John opened Shorty's stall and moved him down to a stall farther away from the scene. He didn't think Shorty needed to see his friend's death.

John latched the gate to the new stall and heard a loud crack followed by shuffling hooves and frantic whinnies from Big. He ran down to the stall to find Big fearfully trying to pull his body away from Fred. One of his eyes fell from his head in a river of tissue and blood.

"What the hell are you doing?" John yelled.

"Putting him out of his misery . . ." said Fred. "Hold him down."

John didn't want to be a part of this and knew Big deserved better, but he also didn't want Big to suffer longer than he had too. Fred started this mess, and John was going to have to help him finish it for Big's sake.

John grabbed a horse blanket and placed it over Big's head, gripping his neck tightly. John could feel the frightened horse's heart beating out of its chest. Angry tears fell from John's eyes, and he wouldn't put it past Fred to put the ax in John's skull while he was at it. He could tell Marie the horse pulled away and he missed . . . it was an accident . . .

The shame John felt for doing this to poor Big brought to mind that he wouldn't care if Fred did knock his block off. He wasn't sure how he could face Shorty, or another man either, after being a part of this.

"Are you ready?" Fred asked.

"Finish it already," said John, who could hear Shorty's hooves pacing excitedly in the stall at the far end of the barn.

The ax fell. Big screamed. John squeezed Big's throat tighter, putting the full weight of his body on top of the horse. Another worthless blow.

The ax fell again. Big screamed, and this time John joined in, in frustration. Big squirmed beneath John's body. The blanket shifted, and John could see the carnage that had become of his constant working companion. John remembered riding him as a young colt out in the pasture, the horse glistened in the sun. He was magnificent.

"Finish it," John yelled.

The ax fell. Big screamed and writhed beneath John. John could smell the coppery scent of blood and could see a pool of Big's life slipping out beneath him. The horse shifted beneath John, and John could feel him weakening.

The ax fell. Big screamed. Shorty's hooves clamored on the sides of the stall that contained him. He cried out to his friend, and Big tried to answer. The squeal that came out of his muzzle didn't sound like a horse but more like a rabbit in the fangs of a cat.

The ax fell. Big screamed. John cried, "What are you doing?"

Fred was silent. He lifted the ax quickly, and Big's blood slid off the blade onto John's face. John could hear the effort in Fred's work. The man puffed and heaved, and John could hear every last bit of strength Fred had being put into the handle. Fred swung the ax down with a loud exhale of breath.

Big mewled like a six hundred–pound kitten. Fred paused. John sobbed. Big lay motionless beneath him. Fred leaned the ax against the side of the stall and turned to leave. He was covered in blood, tissue, and hair. Fred strolled past Shorty's stall, and John could hear the shock and confusion in the silence of Shorty's hooves. John wept. He lay atop the horse and wept until he couldn't produce tears anymore.

At that point, he seethed. His hate for Fred now had legs and a body and a need to be fed.

After Fred had showered off at the water tank, he took his bloodied clothes in to Marie for cleaning.

"What in the world happened?" said Marie.

"We had to put Big down," said Fred.

"How? We don't have a gun," she said.

"We have an ax," he said.

Marie inhaled and covered her mouth with a hand. Her mouth fell open, and she didn't have words to speak.

Marie rushed out to find Shorty in one of the milk cow's stalls and John sitting up against Big's stall covered in tissue and hair and spattered with blood. He was twisting something in his fingers.

"John," she said. "Are you okay?"

John's eyes moved to look at Marie. He stood, lifted the blanket from what remained of Big's head, and said, "What do you think?"

Marie took two steps back, "Oh Lord."

"Seven blows," said John. "That man took seven blows of the ax to kill him when we could've borrowed a gun from Joe Knoell or Uncle Bob or Uncle Bill."

Tears cleaned the blood from John's cheeks in streaks. John moved his gaze toward Shorty, who stood staring his way, pleading for information on his friend.

"Not only did he torture Big. He says he did it to put him out of his misery," said John. "Guess what. Big wasn't in any pain. He was paralyzed in the back—that's all. He felt no pain, Mom. None."

John moved his arm to showcase the result of Fred's solution.

"John," said Marie, "I don't know what to say. I'm sorry."

John picked up the ax and swung it toward the wall. He wanted to release some tension but realized after the fact that he scared Shorty again.

"Can you hand me a blanket," said John. "I'll not walk past Shorty looking this way."

"Sure, John," said Marie, who went to grab another horse blanket for John.

"Here," she said, removing her apron and wiping the carnage from John's face.

"Go shower," she said. "I'll talk to Fred."

"It won't do any good for Big now," said John. "And another thing, I'm not helping dispose of Big either. Fred can bury him on his own."

Covered in the blanket like a Russian immigrant, John strode past Shorty, trying not to look him in the eye. He spent a good deal of time in the shower and had a hard time feeling clean. John scrubbed and scrubbed and couldn't seem to rid himself of Big. As he toweled off, he knew that Big would always be part of him.

By the time John got out of the shower, the day was gone. John didn't feel like doing anything and was dreading milking the cows in the morning next to the scene of the crime.

John approached the house, carrying his soiled clothes, which he dropped next to the porch stairs.

"John," said Marie. "I'll wash those."

"Burn 'em," said John. "They'll never get clean."

Marie knew what John was saying, and she took them inside to the woodstove to dispose of them. She immediately regretted the decision, as the smell of burning flesh and hair filled the air.

John went up to his room to find more clothes. He could hear Fred in the room below him.

"Dear Lord, I ain't never been so sorry for something I've done. God help me I thought he would go down on the first hit. Big sure didn't deserve what he got, and I don't know where to start asking for your mercy. Please, God, throw your grace on me, to wipe me free of this shame I feel. I'm so sorry . . . so sorry . . . so sorry . . ." said Fred, his voice crumbling into tears.

He sobbed quietly and privately, pouring out his anguish to God. It was the only time he could remember crying himself to sleep.

In the morning, from his window, John watched Fred enter the barn. After about fifteen minutes, Fred had pulled Shorty out of the stall, hitched him to Big, and began having Shorty drag Big's body out of the barn, across the yard, and over to the pigpen to be eaten.

John sat on his bed and bawled like a child without his blanket. He put his pillow in his mouth and screamed into it.

He cried himself dry and woke in the middle of the morning. He crept downstairs to find Marie in the kitchen with her Bible.

"John, go back to bed," she said. "Clete and Lee did the milking."

"Did you tell them?" he asked.

"Yes, they are upset about it too."

"Who cleaned it up?" John asked.

"Fred," she said.

"It's about time he cleaned up one of his messes," said John.

Silence filled the room.

"John," Marie said, "I imagine you'll be leaving soon."

"Yeah," said John, "I will." John reached into the cupboard where Marie kept the exiled medicinal whiskey. He grabbed two glasses.

"Do you know what you're going to do," she said.

"Not yet," said John. "Maybe the sugar factory in Geneva, maybe the Marines. I'm not sure."

"Well, there aren't many Marines in Nebraska," Marie said. "Will I ever get to see you?"

"Not a lot," said John. He poured three fingers in each glass.

Marie pursed her lips with sorrow. "You mean an awful lot to this family, John; and whatever you decide, you go with my blessing," Marie said. "However, you are my eldest son, and I love you more than you can understand. I will miss you every day you aren't with me."

John softened. "I know, Mom," he said. "I just can't live here." He picked up one of the glasses and poured it down his throat like a man emerging from a desert.

"I know," said Marie. "I understand."

She reached out and squeezed his hand.

"You always be true to you," she said. "Always."

"Yes, ma'am," he said.

"John," she said. "You don't need whiskey. That never helps anything."

John smiled. "Doctor's orders."

Marie smiled, picking up the glass and lifting it to John as a toast. She sniffed its contents and pulled her twisted face backward.

"I can't, John," she said. "It's just awful."

"Marie," John paused. "You are too strong for whiskey."

John picked up her glass, put it back, cleared his throat as he swallowed her share. He turned from his mother and walked down the long hall. He paused at the screen door and looked out to the barn. He wondered how Shorty slept. He wondered if Shorty would ever trust a man again. He wondered if he would ever be able to erase the scene and the sounds from his own mind. John ascended the stairs and lay down on his bed. He listened to Clete and Lee out in the yard. After a few minutes Uno came to John and leapt up to his side. John put his arm around the dog, and the pair found rest.

⟶ 29 ⟵

Enter through the narrow gate;
for the gate is wide and the way is broad that leads to destruction,
and there are many who enter through it.
For the gate is small and the way is narrow that leads to life,
and there are few who find it.
Matthew 7:13–14

Mondays were wash days for Marie. The kitchen became an inferno in the summertime and comfortable in the winter, as she warmed the water for the gas-powered Maytag wringer washer. She hung wet clothes on the line behind the house all year long. Most of the time, the clothes would freeze before they dried, but no one complained.

Monday was a big work day for Marie, because washing was not an easy chore and because she took advantage of the stove being on and made cinnamon rolls and fresh bread at the same time. The family loved Mondays for that reason. The smell floated throughout the house, and had everyone, including Uno, licking lips and drooling.

Marie would place the pan of rolls and bread on the counter to cool before starting to boil oats for the chicken feed. Beginning this second project would clear the house of the living because the smell was not pleasant. It's funny how everyone found something that needed to be done as soon as oats hit water.

"You should be grateful for this feed, because it keeps us enjoying fried chicken," said Marie.

And that thought would bring the moisture back to the mouths of all.

It was a Monday when the phone rang for Elaine.

Everyone was sitting around the table enjoying cinnamon rolls, and Elaine nervously got up to say hello. Elaine was a treasure. She took great pride in her appearance and in her ability to be graceful. She spoke like an angel when she said, "Hello? This is Elaine McCloud."

She wrung her fingers through the telephone cord. "Oh, yes," she said. "I understand. Yes, next Monday will be fine. Thank you. I'll see you then."

You could have heard a pin drop as she turned around to face the sticky-faced bunch of McClouds.

"I got a job," she said. "You are looking at the new nanny for the Volskie family of Broken Bow."

Cheers broke out, and Angela bounced out of her chair to hug her sister. Lucy followed, and the boys clapped—Lee managed to clap without putting down his cinnamon roll. Being the baby of the family had taught him not to trust his older siblings with sweet treats around.

Lee was worried about this development, because Elaine had been the one to take care of him. She was always there for him, and Lee even admired the way she spoke to Uno. This was going to change his life, and he knew it.

Elaine could see the worry growing on Lee's face.

She came over to him and kneeled down next to his chair.

"Lee," she said. "I won't be around as much as I have been, with this new job."

"Oh," said Lee, wondering what she was going to say next.

"You are a big boy now, and I know you will continue to eat well and take care of Uno every day," she said. "Can I depend on you to be Uno's caretaker?"

"Well," said Lee. "Sure."

"That's a good boy," she said smiling. "I'm going to come home every chance I can to check on you and Uno to see how you're doing."

"Okay," said Lee. "What's Broken Bow like? Are the Volskies nice?"

"They seem very kind," she said. "Their children will be under my care, and they are a lot younger than you are, so they will need a lot of help."

"They will love you, Elaine," Lee said.

"I hope so," she said. "I will miss you every day I'm gone, Lee."

Lee smiled, ready to get back to his cinnamon roll.

Elaine stood and went out to the clothesline to tell Marie the news.

It was less than a week later that the phone rang for Lucy. She went to work in Sargent, Nebraska, at a variety store named Kings. And because Lucy was Clete's assigned caretaker, it was Clete's turn to be thrust into the world of being a "big boy," and Lee could see the transition concerning him.

"You'll be fine," said Lee. "You can help me take care of Uno. It's not an easy job, I can tell you. He is constantly getting into things." Clete agreed Uno was a handful.

And so, the house became a lot quieter in a short amount of time. Everyone missed the girls' quick wit and constant attention. They were great helpers to Marie, and everyone knew Marie was feeling their absence more than anyone.

Angela represented the only remaining girl of the house, since Marie was seen as such an authority figure. You could share anything with Angela and know it would be kept in confidence. Lee could see she was missing the fellowship of her sisters as much, if not more, than the boys.

Angela was still teaching at McCloud School, District 222, which sat on a small acre of land Grandpa Robert McCloud donated for the purpose of education. She had been working longer than any of the other girls, and she seemed to have a large influence on the food the family ate and the generosity of Santa Claus at Christmas.

The first year Angela taught classes, Lee received an excavator to dig dirt with. It had rubber-banded treads and could haul a lot more dirt than you would think for something meant to be a toy. Living in the Dust Bowl armed with an excavator was only a child's dream. Between the appearance of the heavy-duty digging equipment and the

Oklahoma dirt in the yard, Lee enjoyed a constant supply of ground to work in. He wore the machine out in the first year, and thank goodness Santa was paying attention. Replacing the toy became an annual event. The first Christmas after Elaine and Lucy became productive members' of society, Santa had a huge boost in production and distribution. Lee received a BB gun, an excavator, and a doll.

Fred was certain that Santa had taken to the drink. "Boys don't play with dolls."

Lee said, "I do. I like it. She can drive my excavator and ride on Uno."

Fred shook his head.

Lee enjoyed his gifts a great deal. He loved the doll. It was a small girl with brown yarn hair. He imagined it was what Elaine looked like as a young child. It came with a note that said to take very good care of her because she didn't have anyone else. Lee felt honored and it filled some of the void Elaine had left in his days.

And as it turned out, she was a tom boy. She loved riding Uno when Lee could strap her on with a bit of rope. She was also a hard worker. She could ride the excavator for hours without complaining about her fingernails breaking or looking sweaty. They were a good team.

Lee liked to hold her at night when he slept. Since Elaine and Lucy had moved out, more sleeping space became available, so when John and Clete relocated, Uno and Lee were left in the "boys bed" alone. One night Lee woke and was unable to find his doll. He rolled over and held onto Uno, feeling certain she slid under the bed. As daylight crept in through the window, he leaned over to search the floor and realized he was mistaken. He searched his bed. He searched the room. He searched the stairway and made his way down into the kitchen. Fred and Marie sat at the table with coffee and breakfast.

"Good morning, Lee," Marie said.

"Mom, I can't find my doll," Lee said.

Fred lifted a newspaper in front of his face.

Marie inhaled deeply and glared at the printed page held in front of her. She turned her head to Lee and adjusted her look to concern.

"I'm sorry, Lee," she said. "Maybe she got a job like Elaine and Lucy."

"She wouldn't leave without saying goodbye," Lee said. "Can I look in your room?"

"Sure, dear," she said. "Look everywhere. I'll help when I'm done with my coffee."

Uno followed Lee to the room, sniffing the floor. He paused at the door to Fred and Marie's bedroom and changed his direction. Lee noticed him sniff at the woodstove which was roaring with what sounded like a new log. Uno sat in front of the door and raised a paw, batting at the air, being careful not to touch the side of the stove. The dog whimpered and looked toward Lee, who stood in such a way that he couldn't be seen by Marie or Fred.

Lee gazed at Uno realizing his doll wasn't lost. She had been taken and, according to Uno's nose, laid in the flames of the woodstove. Lee sat on the bed. He knew Fred had never liked him playing with a doll but never thought he would stoop to this. He tried not to cry. Tears fell and his nose crinkled up with moisture. He sat as still as he could, looking up at the ceiling and squeezing the tears out of his eyes by squeezing them shut. Uno whimpered.

"Come on, boy," said Lee. "Let's go look outside."

Lee sped out of the bedroom, past his parents, and down the hall to the porch. His driverless excavator sat on the ground, where he left it yesterday. He paused at the screen door; Uno wasn't coming. "Uno," he called a second time.

"Uno," he said again, and the click of the dog's nails echoed down the hall. Before shutting the screen door, Lee saw Marie peek around the wall and down the hall toward him. She looked at him with a sorrowful, apologetic look. Lee knew she couldn't say anything and that his doll would never be spoken of again. He closed the screen door harder than he normally did and walked out into the yard with Uno at his heels.

Lee walked out into the pasture, following the clay path up the hill to the windmill. He found a milk cow to hide behind and cried. The cow gently turned its chewing face toward him and swatted its tail in his direction. Uno sat on the ground leaning on Lee's leg.

He didn't cry very long, just enough to take the edge off. He didn't want to get caught with a face full of tears. After all, Elaine left him in charge of Uno. Lee was a big boy now, and big boys don't cry. Surely Fred had saved Lee from himself again.

Lee thought it was odd that none of his sisters ever asked about his doll when they visited home. He wanted to tell someone of his loss, but he was never given the opportunity. Nine months passed, and there was no mention of Lee's doll again.

When Christmas rolled around, Fred asked Lee what he wanted from Santa. Lee stared at the floor a different man than the one who had lived quietly with the cremation of his favorite toy. Lee pursed his lips and cleared his throat. "I'd like another doll," he said clearly. "One with brown yarn hair who likes to dig in the dirt and be my friend."

Fred exhaled and adjusted his boots to brace himself.

"You think Santa will see to getting me another doll, Fred?" he asked.

Fred took note that it was the first time Lee had ever called him by his first name.

"No, Lee," Fred said. "I don't think Santa gives boys dolls except by accident. He gives boys trains and guns and construction equipment."

"Then I don't need anything from Santa," Lee said as he turned to walk away. He opened the screen door and Uno followed. He didn't know what he had done. Was that back talk? Would there be a belt heading his way? He didn't care. He didn't want anything for Christmas. He was just being honest.

John met him on the porch.

"Whoa," John said. "You look like you're ready for battle."

Lee looked up at John, "I think I just started one."

John stood silently watching him head down the stairs and toward the pasture. Uno trotted alongside him.

John entered the house and saw Fred at the end of the hall.

"Oh, I get it now," said John.

"Good morning, John," Fred said. "I think it's time you found a job."

"You and me both," John said.

Marie exited the bedroom into the middle of their stares.

"For the love of God, can you boys stop it?" Marie said. "I'm done with it."

"John was telling me he was gonna find a job," said Fred.

Marie turned to look at John, "Is that true?"

John thought a moment. "Yes, ma'am," John said. "It's time."

Marie sunk. Fred beamed, stepping into the bedroom.

She looked at John for a moment and then said, "Okay."

John felt a weight lift from his shoulders. "Cows are milked," he said, stomping up the stairs.

He reached the top of the stairs and exhaled. A smile snuck up on him, and his boots stepped a cheerful path to his room.

Sitting on his bed, he could hear Fred in the room below, "We'll be fine, Marie. Clete and Lee can handle it, and I'm tired of John showing my other sons how to disrespect me. Do you know Lee just called me Fred instead of Dad? Where do you think he learned that?"

Marie answered, "Are you surprised? If you weren't so willing to put your responsibilities on your two young boys . . . They have school, and I'll not let them quit like John did. That was a mistake I will take to my grave. John is a wonderful man who has done everything for this family. It's past time for you to step up."

John heard a small scuffle of feet and then a loud crack. He stood from his bed and listened, trying to determine what had happened.

He heard Fred's boots moving down the hall at a determined angry speed. Fred stepped out onto the porch, and John heard the screen bounce three times. The eldest son approached the stairway and snuck quietly down. He moved lightly down the hall and turned into Marie's bedroom. He found her on the floor holding the side of the bed, burying her face in the quilt.

"What happened?" John said.

"Nothing," said Marie. "Go clean up for lunch."

"It's not lunchtime," said John. "What happened?"

Marie pulled her face away from the covers but still wouldn't face John. He scanned the room and found a stool broken on the floor.

"It's okay, John," she said. "Don't worry about it. I lost my temper and threw the stool at him."

John reached down and grabbed her arm, turning her toward him.

"Why do you stay with him?" John asked.

"I'm his wife . . . till death do us part," she said. "I understand why you don't like him, John. I do. But you and Angela knew him when he was young. You knew the whole Fred. The happy-go-lucky Fred. Life has a way of breaking pieces off. You're kidding yourself to think that life hasn't changed me from the bright-eyed lass who stepped off the boat at Ellis."

"He's just no good for you, Mom," said John.

"Neither is whiskey, but I got a prescription for it," she said. "I have never been so ashamed of myself as I am now for throwing that stool."

John stood tugging at his ear, mulling over what her response would be if he congratulated her.

"Life is hard, John; and of all my children, I know you understand that," she said. "There's something harder than life though, and I don't think you've learned that lesson yet."

John sat down on the edge of the bed, wondering where she was taking this conversation.

"Forgiveness," she said. "Forgiveness is the most difficult part of life, and I believe you need to learn how to give it. Jesus bared our sins on the cross and has shown us great mercy. That, John McCloud, is what we are called to do in this life . . . forgive . . . I know Fred loves you, and he doesn't understand your dislike of him. He sees his illness as what keeps him from making you proud and there isn't a damn thing he can do about it," she said. "Won't you soften your heart toward him just for a minute?"

John rubbed his hands together realizing that his presence in the home was no longer a benefit to his mother. He knew he couldn't or wouldn't forgive Fred and that their constant war games tormented her.

"I hear what you are telling me, Mom," John said. "But I still need to leave today. I don't have it in me to forgive him. I'm not sure it'll ever come to that, but I see now that I'm making things harder on you, and I've never wanted that."

Marie reached up to John's knee, and John grabbed her hand.

"I remember when you used to give me a bath in that old wash-tub. Your hands seemed so much softer then," John said. "But I guess my hands have gotten pretty rough over the years, and maybe that's not all . . . I'll go pack up my things."

Marie's face shriveled in pain, and the tears fell freely. John stood, leaving her on the floor with the broken stool. John climbed the stairs possibly for the last time. He packed up his few belongings and took a look around the room. It seemed a sudden departure, and he felt melancholy about his decision. He still felt needed but decided that was his ego; Clete and Lee could handle it. And who knows, perhaps with John gone, Fred may finally take the reins. Only time could tell.

John walked into the room he shared with Lee and Clete when the girls were home, and he sat on the bed. He wasn't sure what his heart was feeling, but he felt guilty about the excitement building inside his chest. He paused for a moment, remembering how he used to tell Clete and Lee stories each night. It was a never-ending saga that kept them on the edge of their seats and put them to sleep all at the same time. He never really knew if he was much of a storyteller, but he loved seeing Clete and Lee smile and twitch when his characters did something exciting or silly.

Looking out the window, he saw Fred pacing from the barn to the shop and back again. He wondered what he was up to and decided he didn't care as long as he was up to something.

Marie walked up to the bedroom door.

"I love you, John," said Marie.

"I love you, Mom," said John standing. "I'll let you know where I land."

Marie smiled. "Will you tell Fred goodbye?" she asked.

John exhaled. "Yeah, I'll be nice."

"Thank you, John," said Marie. "For everything. I don't know what I would've done without you."

John's chest warmed and his temples became hot.

"I hope things turn around," said John. "I really do."

"It's in God's hands," she said.

John walked past her, picked up his sack of clothes, and descended the stairs.

He paused at the bottom and turned up to look at Marie, who remained at the top step. John could see she was trying not to cry.

"Go ahead and cry," John said. "I'll feel bad if you don't."

She smiled and lost it. She glided down to him and gave him a hug.

"You have a way, John," she said.

Lee entered through the screen door and paused at the thickness of air.

"John is leaving us today," said Marie. "He's off to conquer the world."

"What? Today?" Lee asked.

"Yep," said John. "How about you walk me to my car?"

"Well sure, John. Is everything okay?" Lee said.

"Just antsy," said John.

The brothers walked toward the barn, uncertain of what to say. They had never really said goodbye before.

"I'll miss you, John," said Lee.

"I'll miss you, too," said John. "You take care of Mom, okay? She needs someone to make her smile."

"Okay," said Lee. "I'll try."

Uno ran up to join them.

John threw his bag in the car and turned toward Lee.

"Take care of them trees, Lee," he said.

"I will," said Lee.

John scratched Uno's head and sent Marie a last farewell look before turning toward his father, who was keeping busy shoveling hay in Big's former stall.

John approached him unsure of what to say.

"Well, I'm leaving," said John.

"Good luck," said Fred. "I'm sure Clete and Lee can keep things moving along."

John tugged at his ear. "Well, good luck to you," said John. "I know we haven't always seen eye to eye, and I'm awful sorry we caused Marie the grief. I hope things fall into place for the family with me out of the way."

Fred leaned the pitchfork against the stall wall and stepped forward toward John. "You were never in the way," said Fred. "You mean a lot to this family, myself included."

Fred extended a hand to John, who stared at it. After a moment, Fred began to pull his hand back, obviously disappointed; and John reached forward to shake it on the return. Fred smiled, and John made note of how smooth Fred's hands seemed compared to his mom's.

"Okay then," said John.

"Goodbye, John," said Fred. "Let your mama know where you are. You know she'll worry."

"I will," he said.

John tousled Lee's hair as he passed.

"See ya' later, kid," John said.

Lee was beginning to tear up. "Bye," he said.

John slid into the vehicle and steered it down the lane. At the end of the lane, he had a choice to turn left or right. Left would take him to Anselmo. Right would go to Merna.

He turned left, wondering what the hell he was gonna do at the next intersection.

Marie watched the dust from John's car cloud up in his wake.

"He'll be fine," she said.

"I know," said Lee. "John is always strong."

Marie nodded, fighting back tears, and said, "Let's go."

"Okay," said Lee.

Marie sat down in the porch chair. Uno approached her and lay his head in her lap.

"What am I gonna do with them," said Marie.

Uno licked his lips and sat down. He pulled his ears back to his head and exhaled a sigh that said it all, "How the hell should I know?"

The dust cloud settled on the path to Anselmo, where John decided to fill up with gas on the outskirts. As he pulled out of the gas station, he paused. He turned his blinker on to head west. It clicked and clicked in John's ear until he spun the wheel east and gave it some gas. At the last second, he returned to his original plan and corrected the wheel west. He floored the gas pedal and committed. Three miles in, he decided he had made a grievous error, because facing the setting sun was difficult. He squinted for an hour before he felt his face return to a normal, relaxed position.

The cool night air brushed through him and cleansed him of the day's drama. His favorite sound, the cicadas, bid him farewell, and their song was damn beautiful. The farm boy had never experienced the allegro and crescendo of their harmony from a moving vehicle, and the way the speed and air played against his ear was seductive. He inhaled the chill of the Sandhills and bid his first love adieu.

Rolling down the window, he rested his left arm on the door frame and let his fingers glide out into the darkening sky. The excitement of the road energized him, and he felt as if he could drive all night. His empty stomach gurgled and hissed. He was a practical man and knew food was critical to the success of his trip. He found himself imagining Marie's fried chicken crackling in the greasy skillet.

Less than ninety minutes from home and with his mouth watering, he pulled into a cafe.

"Where you headed?" the waitress asked.

"Hell if I know," said John. "Any recommendations?"

"California," she said. "It's warm all year long."

"Sounds good to me," said John. "Got a map?"

"There's one on the wall near the front," she said.

"Thank you," he said. "I'll have the fried chicken and a coffee."

"Sure thing, sweets," she said, turning to the kitchen window. "Order in!"

John scanned the restaurant and realized it was a lowly crowd, himself included. Trying not to feel discouraged about stopping ninety minutes into his journey, he realized leaving home on an empty stomach was not a good strategic move.

But still . . . it felt good. Really good . . . Looking at his hands holding the coffee cup, he realized he was a mess. His hands were stiff, and his skin was rough and calloused. There were probably still bits of Oklahoma under his fingernails, which he decided was a good souvenir. He was short on money due to his sudden departure and decided he would head west as far as he could afford and then figure out what to do next.

The world was John's at last. He swore over that weak cup of joe that Fred would never see John's forgiveness. As he waited for his order, he decided to check out the map the waitress spoke of. As he approached the front of the restaurant, his eye caught a poster advertising for the US Marines. The soldier, pictured in a faultless dress blue uniform stood tall with hands crossed behind his back. The impressive bearing and confidence shown from his pores, expression and stance. Braided gold cords hung from his left shoulder encircling his arm. John thought this man was a true hero... he had class, strength, discipline and, a steady income ... all very attractive features at the moment.

"Order up," the cook said, dinging a bell.

"Come and get it sweetheart," the waitress said waving John back to his seat.

John turned on his heel toward the stool and asked the server if he would look good in blue.

"Oh yeah," she said. "I can see you in blue showing off those eyes."

John nodded his head, "Well that settles it," he said. "Blue is my color."

He took his seat and leaned into his plate for a whiff of the chicken. Disappointed, he anticipated a lack of flavor.

"That's what ya get when you rush off," he said to himself. "A dry, tasteless bird."

"Everything okay," asked the waitress.

"Never better," John said as he worked to chew the chicken. "Never better."

"Are you sure?" she said.

"To tell ya the truth," he said. "This is the worst chicken I've seen in all my years but I'm gonna eat it, enjoy it, and remember it for the rest of my days as the first chicken of the rest of my life. It all gets better from here."

The waitress raised an eyebrow, "As long as you're happy honey, I'm happy."

"I'm happy," he said. "Damn happy."

She laughed, "Did you decide where you going?"

"Eventually," John said. "I gotta make some money along the way but I know where I'll end up. . . that's all that matters."

"Godspeed," she said.

"Godspeed," he muttered.